NEVER LETTING GO

CARNIVALE CHRONICLES

SHERYL LISTER

ABOUT NEVER LETTING GO

When journalist Asia Montgomery took her wedding vows, she meant them. Yet, somewhere along the way, things changed. With her marriage crumbling all around her and her trust shattered, she fears it may be too late to save it. She takes refuge at a tropical resort to figure out her next steps, but doesn't count on Jamal following her there...or his persistence.

Jamal Montgomery knew his wife, Asia, was the only woman he'd ever want. He has no intention of giving up on them, but gets the surprise of his life when he comes home early from a business trip and finds her gone. The tenacious attorney is determined to win her back and goes after her. Now everything they've built is hanging in the balance. Jamal and Asia will have to fight to rediscover the love they once shared and the passionate dreams yet to be fulfilled.

To love, marriage & keeping it together

ACKNOWLEDGMENTS

My Heavenly Father, thank You for Your sufficient grace.

To my husband, Lance: your love, support and encouragement is what keeps me going.

Thank you to my friends and family for your consistent support.

To my Book Euphoria sisters, I love you ladies!

To all of my readers: thank you from the bottom of my heart.

Nicole Falls, your editorial guidance is priceless. Thank you.

DEAR READER

Dear Reader,

I am excited to be part of another fabulous Book Euphoria anthology and hope you enjoy the Carnivale Chronicles. You met Jamal and Asia Montgomery in Her Passionate Promise (Women of Park Manor) and got a hint of the discord in their marriage. Now they take center stage and things have gotten worse. Will they be able to make it work? Hmm... You'll have to read to find out.

As always, I look forward to hearing from you. Until next time...

Love & Blessings,
Sheryl

CHAPTER 1

"*D*on't stop, Jamal."

Jamal Montgomery had no intention of stopping. Not now with her feminine muscles clenching him so tightly and her heels clasped around his back. He grabbed her hips and guided her to move faster. Her nails dug into his shoulders and each time she arched upward, Jamal thrust downward to meet and match her strokes, going deeper each time. He could feel himself teetering on the brink of his control, but he wasn't ready for it to end. His body trembled slightly and he closed his eyes as the sensations intensified. "I could stay inside you all night," he murmured. Their blended cries echoed in the otherwise silent room. He dipped his head, latched onto an erect nipple and she called his name. Jamal kissed his way back to her mouth and moved his tongue in and out, mimicking the movements of his lower body.

"Yes! Right there." Abruptly, she broke off the kiss and moaned as she climaxed all around him.

It was her second one of the night and the more pleasure he could draw from her, the more it fueled his own. This was how it had always been between them. He lifted her legs higher and plunged deeper and deeper, bringing her to another hard, shuddering climax that made her scream his name. She was still catching her breath when he shifted positions, turning her over and entering her from behind. He held her closer and thrust deeply. Groaning with pleasure, he moved faster and faster until his orgasm roared through him with such force, it shook his entire body and tore a hoarse shout from his throat. Before he could recover, he came again in a rush of pleasure that made bright lights flash behind his eyes. His head hung limply and his breaths came in short gasps. As their breathing slowed, Jamal rolled to his side. Before he could pull her into his embrace, she slid off the bed. "Asia?"

"I'll be right back," she mumbled and went into the bathroom.

He fell back against the pillows and let out a frustrated sigh. Just like the last two times they'd made love, instead of laying together, Asia had left the bed as if it were on fire. He missed the intimacy they'd previously shared—the gentle touches and tender kisses that usually came afterward. Tonight had been just…sex. He didn't want sex, he wanted love and everything that came with it. The day they took their vows, he had promised to never let anything come between them and to never let go of their love and she'd done the same. Yet, less than three years later, they had broken those promises.

Jamal must have drifted off because the next he knew, his alarm was blaring and shards of sunlight streamed through the closed blinds. He shut off the noise, turned over and scrubbed a hand down his face. He was in bed alone. Again. The slight indentation in her pillow was the only indication that his wife had slept there at all. He listened, thinking she might be in the bathroom, but when he got up and went to the door, he found it empty. His first thought was to find her and try to talk, but he nixed the idea. Jamal had a long day ahead of him at the office. He and his friend and colleague, Eric Dawson were heading up a class action lawsuit filed by residents of an apartment complex due to the owner's negligence in addressing a mold issue, and Jamal couldn't afford any distractions.

Instead, he showered, dressed, then went downstairs. He stopped short upon seeing Asia standing at the counter, dicing up some fruit. She had on a skimpy tank and sleep shorts that stopped just below the curve of her butt that exposed more of her caramel skin than they covered. It brought to remembrance the way he'd caressed and gripped her shapely backside as he took them both on a trip to ecstasy. Jamal's groin stirred and he pushed the image aside. He draped his suit coat over a barstool and set his briefcase down. "Good morning."

Asia glanced at him over her shoulder. "Morning. I made coffee." She placed the medley of melon, pineapples, and strawberries into a bowl, rinsed everything and then stuck the dirty dishes into the dishwasher.

Jamal came up behind her and slid an arm around her waist. Trailing kisses along her neck and bare shoulder, he murmured, "Let's have dinner tonight."

"I...I can't. I have to work late."

He dropped his hand slowly and stepped back. "Come on, baby. You've worked late every night for the past two weeks."

Her eyes flashed in anger. "I'm not the only one who works late, Jamal, so don't try to lay all the blame at my door."

"Asia, I'm not blaming you for anything. I just want to spend time with my wife. How is that a bad thing?" For a split second, her features softened, but it was gone so fast it could have been just wishful thinking on his part.

"I need to get ready for work. I'll see you later." Asia stood there a moment, as if trying to decide something. Finally, she came up on tiptoe and gave him a quick kiss, then walked out.

Things must be at an all-time low if she has to think about kissing me goodbye, Jamal mused while pouring a cup of coffee. He stuck an English muffin in the toaster and peeled two of the eggs he'd boiled last night while waiting. When everything was done, he took his plate and coffee to the bar. As he ate, he checked his emails. He'd left the office yesterday evening at six and had cleared out his inbox. Now, twelve hours later, he had thirty-two messages waiting. He shook his head. "Do these people ever sleep?" Seeing nothing that couldn't wait until he got to the office, he finished his breakfast and drove to the law firm. The warm early June temperatures made him wish he'd chosen a career that didn't require long sleeves and ties every day, but he loved his job, so he cranked up the air conditioner and the music, and made himself comfortable.

When he arrived, Jamal spoke to the legal assistant who worked with him and two other attorneys before continuing the few steps to his office. He rifled through the stack of messages on his desk, put them aside and powered up his computer. The large firm employed thirty-eight attorneys, twelve paralegals, and a large administrative staff, and ran like a well-oiled machine.

"Morning. Got a minute?"

His head came up. "Hey, Eric. Come on in." He had met Eric Dawson in law school and they ended up working at the same firm. He studied his friend. Eric had gotten married almost a year ago after knowing his wife for only two months and Jamal had never seen him smile so much. "How's Kathi?"

A broad smile covered Eric's face. "Pregnant."

Jamal came to his feet and stuck out his hand. "Congrats, man. I'm happy for you two." A pang of envy hit him. He and Asia had talked about having children, but the last time he'd mentioned it, she said she didn't think the timing was right.

"Thanks. Maybe you and Asia can come over so we can celebrate."

His smile faded. "That's probably not going to happen." Although, Asia and Eric's wife, Kathi, had bonded instantly, lately, he'd declined their dinner invitations because he was tired of putting on a front.

"Still having problems? I thought things were getting better."

"So did I, but over the past couple of weeks, it seems the only time we're together for more than five minutes is in bed."

"I'm really sorry. If there's anything I can do, let me know."

"If you have a magic wand that can turn the time back to two years ago, I'll take it."

Eric chuckled. "I wish. As soon as I finish going through my emails, we can look over the second interviews from the apartment complex tenants."

Jamal nodded. "I need to finish mine, too." He glanced at the clock on the wall. "Thirty minutes?"

"That works."

As soon as Eric left, he opened up his emails, but his mind kept straying to his wife. He had no idea how to fix the mess that was his marriage, but he wouldn't give up. He *couldn't* give up.

Asia Montgomery dropped down into her office chair and blew out a long breath. She had no idea how she and Jamal had become so distant. Were they growing apart? Admittedly, the long hours they both had been spending at the office were a contributing factor, but somehow, it felt like something else. Something she couldn't put her finger on, as yet. She sent her two friends, Dena and Marcia a text to see if they could meet for lunch. Asia needed to talk this through with someone other than her husband.

Focusing her mind, she opened the file containing the research and notes for her article on housing discrimination and pored through them, making annotations here and there. It would be her biggest assignment and she hoped it afforded her the opportunity to do more in the way of real journalism and put her degree to work. *Divine Living & Travel* magazine had been in existence for just over a decade and had grown steadily in that time, becoming a household name.

No matter how she tried, Asia couldn't get Jamal and his request to have dinner together out of her mind. Maybe she should have agreed. Yes, she loved her husband, but at this point, she didn't have a clue what to say. And she was afraid of what he might say. Pushing her personal life aside, she went back to the articles. Half an hour later, she gave up and decided a cup of hot tea might help. As soon as she stood, her cell chimed. Asia read the texts from her friends confirming they were available for lunch. She sent back the name of the café near her office and continued to the break room.

"Hey, Asia," her co-worker, Janelle called out.

"Hey." She grabbed a cup and rifled through the tea choices, settling on passionfruit mango. "How's your week going?" She poured hot water and dunked the tea bag a couple of times.

"It's going. It would be better if I could write something other than these little pieces on comparing brands of whatever products." Janelle made a face. "I didn't spend all that time in school for this crap."

"I hear you. Have you looked elsewhere?"

"Yeah, but there isn't much out there right now, unless it's freelancing, and I need a steady paycheck."

Asia studied the forty-something woman, whose light brown skin looked as tired as she sounded. Janelle was nice enough, but she was late to work by ten to fifteen minutes at least twice a week, citing one excuse or another. And she hardly ever turned in her assignments on time. Asia knew Janelle wasn't happy, but had to wonder if that had anything to do with the projects she'd been assigned. One thing was true, however. She had also done some research on jobs in the area and found only a few, and none of them had piqued Asia's interest. Though the magazine billed itself as lifestyle and travel, Asia had yet to be assigned to cover anything that could be categorized as *lifestyle*. And she hadn't traveled anywhere outside of the city. Something had to give, and soon. She added sweetener to her tea, stirred and took a careful sip.

Janelle disposed of her cup. "What are you working on now?"

"An article on housing discrimination." Her supervisor had asked her to discuss the current crisis, but Asia planned to include the country's history of discrimination, real estate's part in the fiasco, as well as interview a few people. It could go one of two ways in her mind—her boss would toss the article out and call it an act of insubordination or applaud Asia's dedication to going above and beyond. She hoped for the latter. "And I need to get back to it. Good luck."

"You, too."

The women left the room and went in opposite directions. Determined not to end up feeling like Janelle, Asia stuck her earbuds in, powered up her favorite kick-butt playlist and starting writing. She only had three weeks to get it done and she planned to make it the best one yet. She was so lost in her task that it took a moment for the soft chiming of her cell phone to register. She searched under the mounds of paper on her desk until she found it. "Hey, Dena."

"Are you standing us up? You're the one who invited us to lunch."

She frowned. "What?"

"You said twelve-thirty and it's fifteen minutes past that now."

Asia jumped up from her chair and glanced up at the wall clock. "Oh, shoot. Sorry. On my way." She quickly saved and closed the file on her laptop, tried to bring some semblance of order to her desk, then rushed out. Thankfully, the café was a short five-minute walk.

Marcia waved when Asia entered. "Over here."

She made her way to where her friends sat and slid into the empty chair. "I'm so sorry. I got caught up on the article I'm working on." She picked up the menu. "Have you guys ordered yet."

"Yes," Dena said. "So, what's up? You don't usually call on a Wednesday and ask to have lunch. We usually have to tie you down three months in advance to get on your schedule."

Asia waited until placing her order before answering. "Jamal and I are having problems and I don't know what to do."

Marcia raised a brow. "You think he's cheating?"

The notion had crossed her mind once or twice, but only fleetingly. "I don't think so."

"You sure? As fine as he is, I know women are probably trying to throw their panties at him on the regular."

The first time Asia had introduced them to Jamal, Marcia had called him *sinfulicious*, a combination of sinfully sexy and divinely delicious. Asia agreed. The two women had been with Asia the day she'd met him and teased her about not being to take her eyes off him. She still couldn't. Even with the turmoil between them, the man could still turn her inside out and had done exactly that last night.

Dena shot Marcia a glare. "Shut up, Marcia." She gave Asia's arm a reassuring touch. "Honey, Jamal loves you and wouldn't cheat on you. I know you love him, too. What's going on?"

"I honestly don't know. We used to laugh, talk and spend time together doing nothing. Now, we're working late all the time and barely talking." Both had canceled lunches and dinners, and each time seemed to chip away at the bond the two of them had forged from the moment they'd met.

"Hmm...working late," Marcia said. "Alone?"

"Marcia, you're not helping." Dena waved a dismissive hand. "Don't listen to her. Sounds like you both need to take some time to figure out how to reconnect."

Marcia shrugged. "I'm just sayin'. But I know y'all love each other, so I hope you can work it out."

Their food arrived and they ate in silence for a few minutes, giving Asia time to digest the conversation. She tried to focus more on Dena's advice more than Marcia's, however. Over the meal, she shared more about her fears and promised to try to meet Jamal halfway.

By the time Asia made it back to the office, she felt much better and planned to see if she and Jamal could have dinner on Friday night. Smiling for the first time in days, she turned her attention back to her work. It was after eight when she arrived home and she found Jamal at the kitchen table scribbling furiously on a legal pad.

"Hi."

His head came up. "Hey. How was your day?"

"Long. Looks like yours has been the same."

Jamal ran a hand down his face and stretched. "It has."

Asia hated the stilted exchange they were having, as if they'd just met. "Um…you mentioned us having dinner. Is Friday a good day?"

He studied her for a lengthy moment. "It will be."

She nodded and started from the room.

"Asia?"

She paused. He stood, came over to her and trailed a finger down her cheek, then tilted her chin and kissed her softly.

"No matter what, don't ever forget that I love you."

Her heart started pounding.

He smiled faintly, pivoted on his heel and strode out.

She braced her hands on the counter and bowed her head as a tear slid down her cheek. She loved him, too and prayed they could work it out.

$\mathscr{F}$riday morning, Asia breezed through the office doors feeling better than she had in a long time. She responded to her emails, then made preparations for her meetings with two people who had been discriminated against. Armed with their addresses, she let the administrative assistant know she would be out of the office on assignment until lunch.

"Don't forget about the staff meeting this afternoon at two."

"I saw the email and I'll be there." She couldn't figure out why her boss decided to call a staff meeting at the end of the week, and in the afternoon. Asia drove to the first house located in a nice neighborhood in Culver City. Her knock was answered by a middle-aged African American man. "Mr. Gibson?"

He gave her questioning look. "Yes."

"I'm Asia Montgomery. We spoke on the phone."

"Oh, yes." Mr. Gibson unlocked the screen and held it open for her to enter. "Please, come in."

"Thank you."

"We can talk in the living room." He gestured her to a comfortable looking sofa. "Let me get my wife."

While he was gone, Asia withdrew a pen and notebook from her bag, along with her phone. With the couple's permission, she activated the voice memo function to be doubly sure she didn't miss anything. He returned a minute later with his smiling wife. Asia stood and extended her hand. "It's nice to meet you, Mrs. Gibson. I want to thank you both for taking time out of your schedules to speak with me." A friend of hers had told her about the couple's plight.

"No problem," Mr. Gibson said. "What would you like to know?"

"As I said on the phone, I'm a journalist for *Divine Living & Travel* magazine. I'm writing an article on housing discrimination and would like to include true accounts. Would you be comfortable sharing your experience with me?"

"Of course," Mrs. Gibson answered.

Rather than ask more specific questions first, Asia opted to have them just share what occurred when they purchased the house three years ago.

Mr. Gibson, a dentist, started. "One of my colleagues bought a house in this area and when Thea and I visited him and his wife, we liked the area, as well. I asked and he gave me the name of his realtor. We were already preapproved for our budget, so I figured it would be easy—we'd look at houses in our chosen area, find the right one and be done."

Asia paused in taking notes. "It didn't work out that way?"

Mrs. Gibson took up the tale. "Not at all. First of all, that woman gave us a listing that had about four houses on it, and none of them were in the area of Culver City we asked for. All of the neighborhoods were rundown. When I asked her about it, she said she thought we might like to be in familiar surroundings—meaning all Black folks—and that the people were very friendly." She rolled her eyes. "Like maybe we didn't know about all the problems and crime."

"What made it worse," Mr. Gibson continued, "was that she'd told Roger the total opposite and even suggested that he research the crime activity in the area for safety reasons."

"Did you feel as if the realtor was trying to steer you in away from more affluent neighborhoods?"

Mrs. Gibson folded her arms. "She tried to steer us away from predominately *white* neighborhoods."

"How did you handle it?"

"At first, I thought it was an accident, but after about the third house, I knew she was doing it deliberately. We fired her and found someone else. When he showed us this house, I was sold," she added with a laugh as she glanced around the elegantly furnished room.

"You'd think with us being in the twenty-first century, we'd be past that, but evidently not." Mr. Gibson shook his head in disgust.

Asia agreed wholeheartedly. She read over her notes and asked a few more questions. She stood. "I want to thank you again for seeing me." She handed them her card. "If you think of anything else, please give me a call."

Mr. Gibson walked Asia to the door. "I appreciate you listening to our story. We tried to complain to the real estate company, but they pretty much ignored us. I hope something comes of your article. This shouldn't still be happening to decent folks."

"So do I." She said her goodbyes and made the twenty-minute drive to Santa Monica for her next interview. The one thing Asia had never gotten used to was LA's traffic and the ten or fifteen extra minutes it took to go seven miles.

Once again, she was given a similar story where an African American couple was shown houses only in predominately minority neighborhoods. Asia also learned that one real estate agent told them that the upscale Santa Monica area where they ended up purchasing was too expensive for their budget, yet had shown the homes to their friends, who happened to be a white couple with a smaller purchasing budget. Asia thanked the young couple and left. She stopped for a salad and took it back to her office and worked through her lunch.

Later that afternoon, she and the rest of the staff filed into the large conference room for the staff meeting. Her boss swept in and took a seat at the head of the table. The tense set of the woman's face gave Asia pause. In the four years that Asia had worked there, she had only seen Lori Tyler upset a handful of times. Everyone seemed to sense the tension and the loud buzz around the room dissipated to a few low murmurs.

Lori clasped her hands together on the table. "I apologize for the short notice and won't keep you long. Phillip Hooper will no longer be working with us."

The murmurings grew louder, with everyone speculating on Phillip's departure. The way Lori announced it made it appear as if the choice hadn't been his. She tuned back in to her boss' voice.

"That means a few things. First, there will be a senior writer position opening up that we'll be looking to fill within the next few weeks. Second, his article will be pulled from this month's edition of the magazine and we need to fill the space. Asia?"

Asia's head popped up.

"I've decided to move up the schedule for your piece on housing discrimination. Instead of being included in next month's issue, it'll replace Phillip's in this month's. I need the final copy next Friday. Will that be a problem?"

Yes! she wanted to shout. The timeline didn't give her

much time to finish and she saw more late days in her future. "No problem."

"I'd like to talk to you before you leave."

"Alright." As soon as the word left her mouth, she remembered that she and Jamal were supposed to be having dinner.

When she got back to her office, she sent him a text explaining. It took almost forty minutes for his one-word reply: *Fine.* Asia lowered her head to the desk. *I can't do this.*

Jamal stood with his hands shoved deep into his pockets staring out of his fourth-floor office window at the ocean in the distance. He had been distracted ever since reading Asia's text canceling their dinner. He tried to give her the benefit of the doubt because he, too, had gotten stuck with a change in schedule and had to work late, but it seemed that work was interfering with their relationship more often than not these days. Lately, Jamal had started bringing his work home, in an effort to get home earlier. His plan was for him and Asia to have dinner together, work a couple of hours and leave time at the end of the day for them. She'd told him she would try to do the same. However, it hadn't been working. He was the only one making it home before eight o'clock. It made him speculate on whether she wanted out.

"You're going to mess around and be here until midnight if you keep daydreaming."

He rotated slightly to see Eric leaning against the doorframe with a smirk on his face. "Go to hell."

Eric pushed off the wall and entered the office. "Looks like you beat me there."

"Believe me, it feels like that's exactly where I am. Asia has to work late and canceled dinner again." Maybe it was all in his mind, but it seemed like the cancellations were occurring more frequently. This one stung, but nothing like last year on their anniversary when he'd cooked dinner for her, ran a bubble bath and spread rose petals on their bed. She'd gotten home far beyond the time she had told him. By then, both the dinner and bathwater were cold and he'd gone to bed.

"Cut her some slack. We have to work late sometimes, too."

"I know that and I'm trying. I suggested we get home early, eat together, then work, so we could at least spend a few minutes talking." Jamal faced the window again. "She agreed, but hasn't done it once in the past two weeks. I don't know what I'll do if I lose her."

Eric came and stood next to Jamal. "You're not going to lose her, man. All couples go through ups and downs, and you two will get through this."

"I hope so. Did you want something?"

"Just wanted to confirm our meeting with the complex owner and his attorney next Monday."

He leaned over and brought up his calendar. "I have it down for ten in the morning."

"They want to change it to eleven. Will that be a problem?"

"No." Jamal clicked a few keys and changed the time. "What are you doing tonight?"

"Kathi is hanging out with Faith and the band is playing again at Infuse Rhythm Lounge at eight. Calvin and I decided to do dinner first around six-thirty. There may be one or two more band members, if they show. You're welcome to join us."

"Sounds good." He could drown his sorrows and hear great music all at the same time. And it beat going home to an empty house. He checked his watch. That gave him an hour to finish up and be out the door by five-thirty. He figured with traffic, it would take at least forty-five minutes to get to Santa Monica. If he was lucky. "I'll meet you there."

Eric nodded. "Later."

Jamal went back to his desk and opened the file for the brief he'd been writing. Moments later, his thoughts strayed back to Asia. He picked up the phone.

"Hey."

"Hey, baby. I know you're going to be working a little late, but what about meeting me at *Infuse Rhythm* to see Eric's band at eight?"

"I don't know, Jamal. I really have to get this article finished in the next few days, since Lori changed the timeline."

"I know, but you need a break. We can watch the show and, you can work at home afterward."

There was a pause, then Asia said, "Not tonight, okay? Let's plan for next weekend, if they're playing. I have to go. Lori's ready to meet with me."

She hung up before he could say anything else. Jamal tossed the phone on his desk and buried his head in his hands. Asia was trying to get a promotion and he wanted her to have it. In the meantime, he kept convincing himself things would get better soon.

Just as he'd predicted, it had taken almost an hour to get to the restaurant. Rather than search for parking, he turned the car over to the valet. Inside, the hostess greeted him with a big smile.

"Welcome. We have open seating at the bar, or would you prefer a table?"

"Actually, Eric Dawson is expecting me."

Her smile widened. "Well, follow me. Any friend of Eric's is a friend of mine."

Jamal chuckled and trailed the woman, whose name tag said Della.

She glanced back. "You wouldn't happen to be single? I have a niece who'd be perfect for you."

"No, not single. Married."

She placed the menu on the table where Eric sat with another man, the keyboardist for the band. She looked Jamal up and down. "Pity. Enjoy your evening."

"Thanks." He sat. "Hey, Calvin. How's it going?"

Calvin grinned. "Better than you, looks like."

"Glad you made it," Eric said. "Ms. Della trying to fix you up with a niece?"

"How did you know?"

"She does it to everyone."

Jamal had been there twice with Asia, but he guessed with the number of people she ran into daily, she wouldn't remember that fact. He picked up the menu. "Have you guys ordered?"

"Yep. Just did." Eric raised his hand to get the server's attention. "Do you know what you want?"

He was torn between the steak and the salmon, but decided on the fish. He had been trying to reduce his red meat intake. His mother suffered from high blood pressure and she had made similar dietary changes with good results. Jamal already worked in a stressful environment and didn't need to add any other worries. His current situation at home was enough to send his pressure through the roof.

Jamal chatted with the men while eating and when they left for the stage, he decided to sit at the bar, instead of taking up a table. He slid onto the last stool in the crowded space and ordered a whiskey on the rocks. He let the low burn of the drink and the smooth sounds of the band soothe his mind.

"Hey, Jamal."

He pinched the bridge of his nose. *I don't need this tonight.*

He shifted on the stool to face the woman standing next to him. "Stephanie."

"Fancy meeting you here."

More like you were outside my office listening to my conversation with Eric. "Not really." Stephanie Carlson worked as a paralegal in their office. They had gone out for drinks after work twice before he'd met Asia four years ago. He hadn't viewed the encounters as anything other than coworkers relaxing at the end of the day, and had been clear about his intentions from the start. Apparently, Stephanie had missed the memo, or ignored it completely, but he'd had to reiterate that he didn't play where he worked. He wasn't her boss, per se, however, the power element was still there and he'd worked too hard to throw it away for a meaningless fling that could potentially turn into a sexual harassment nightmare.

Stephanie gave him a flirty smile. "Aren't you going to offer to buy a girl a drink?"

Jamal eyed her. Not wanting to deal with her antics, he tossed back the rest of his drink and stood. "I think you can handle that on your own. Have a good evening." His marriage was in enough trouble without adding more shit to the pile.

CHAPTER 3

A week later, Asia sat at her desk reading over her article one last time. She was pleased with how it had turned out and hoped Lori felt the same way. Taking a deep breath, she typed a short email, attached the document and hit the send button. She went through the photos from the art and design department and chose a few potential ones she thought would work well with the piece if Lori approved it. Her cell rang and she saw Jamal's name on the display. "Hey."

"Hey. Just checking to see if you're still coming to the firm's annual banquet tonight."

"I am." She hated the skepticism she heard in his voice, but couldn't blame him. He'd left before she'd gotten up due to an early conference call, so they hadn't talked. "I thought about trying to go home first, but with traffic, didn't want to chance it, so I brought my dress with me and I'll meet you there. Cocktail hour starts at six-thirty, right?" He worked ten minutes from their Manhattan Beach home, while her commute to Long Beach took more than half an hour. She could cut her time in half if she drove straight to the swanky Beverly Hills hotel where the banquet was being held.

"Yes. I'll see you there. Love you."

"Love you, too."

"Knock, knock."

Asia placed the phone on the desk. "Hey, Janelle." Janelle reached behind her and closed the door and Asia lifted a brow. "What's up?"

Janelle came closer and spoke in hushed tones. "Did you hear the reason Phillip was fired?"

"No." She had been so busy trying to get her stuff done, she hadn't had time listen to the gossip mill. It did confirm her suspicion that he hadn't left of his own free will.

"I talked to Myra and she said he'd been padding his articles with information that wasn't true to make them more sensationalized."

"Why would he do that? He had a great writing style and was one of the most experienced writers here."

She shrugged. "I guess he wanted that top spot right below Lori."

Asia shook her head. "How did he get caught?"

"One of the staff writers overheard him offering to pay a guy he knew to inflate some information on that nutrition article. Apparently, the guy worked with a dietitian, but wasn't one and the one piece of information he gave turned out to be wrong."

Their boss and the editing staff were diligent about fact checking and she didn't understand why Phillip didn't think someone would catch the slip-up.

"With him gone and Alejandro leaving, that leaves two spots open. I need to get myself together so I can move up."

Asia smiled. "Good for you."

"I'm working on an opinion piece on fad diets. With as

many of them as I've tried, I'm definitely an expert," Janelle added with a laugh. "It's only 500-750 words, but I'll take it."

"You're going to knock it out of the park." She wanted the woman to succeed. There was more than enough room at the top for both of them.

"Thanks, Asia. You're one of the few people here who supports other writers. I hope you get one of the senior writer positions."

"I appreciate that." She rubbed her hands together. "I guess we'd better get moving if we plan to take over the world."

Janelle's laughter filled the office as she left.

Smiling, Asia went back to her task. At five, she shut down her computer and retrieved her toiletry bag so she could freshen up before changing.

"Oh, good. You're still here."

"Hi, Lori." Had she finished reading the article? She studied her boss but the woman's features were unreadable.

"I need to see you in my office, please."

"Sure." Lori smiled faintly and walked out, leaving Asia to follow. Asia hoped the conversation wouldn't take long. Belatedly, she wished she had a moment to send a message to Jamal, just in case she ended up being a few minutes late.

Once there, Lori gestured to a chair. "Have a seat." Then she rounded the desk and sat in her own.

Asia perched on the edge of the seat and wrung her hands. She bounced her knee, a nervous habit and clamped a hand over them, willing herself to relax.

"I read your piece on housing discrimination and loved it. I was impressed by your foresight to include the country's history, as well as how the real estate market contributes to this ongoing problem."

"Thank you." She was amazed by her ability to respond so

calmly when she wanted to jump up and down like a kid at Christmas.

"I was particularly intrigued by the first accounts."

Unlike Phillip, Asia made sure each couple signed a release form that included their personal information. If anyone had questions, they could easily contact the source. "They were very forthcoming with the information."

"This will work nicely in this month's issue." She continued to praise the piece.

Asia discreetly peeked at her watch. If she left within the next ten minutes, she could still get there by the seven o'clock dinner time.

"Since you started here four years ago, you've grown to become one of our best writers."

"I hope to continue to grow as a writer."

Lori passed Asia a folder. "To help you along, I'd like for you to cover the Chi-Flavor Afro-Caribbean Carnivale in Chicago. It'll be the third weekend in July."

Oh. My. Goodness. I'm going on a travel assignment! She opened the folder and scanned the top sheet. "That's next month."

"Your flight, hotel, car rental and daily food allowance will all be included."

Grinning, Asia said, "This is great. I'm looking forward to it." She wasn't familiar with the festival, but she would be by the time she arrived in Chicago. Lori went over the details—taking photos, interviewing the headlining artists and attendees, capturing the flavor of the event.

"You can read the information in your packet and let me know if you have any questions next week."

"Okay. I appreciate you trusting me with this assignment."

Lori stood and smiled. "It was a no-brainer. Have a good weekend."

She followed suit. "You, too." Asia almost skipped down

the hallway to her office. She picked up her phone and sent a group text to her girls, complete with a screaming emoji. She couldn't wait to share the news with Jamal. *Jamal!* Asia's gaze flew to the clock on the wall. She cursed. She was supposed to be there like...*now.*

Asia sprinted out of the office to the bathroom to clean up, then back to her office. She quickly changed into her dress and stuck her feet into her heels. She nearly tripped in her haste to leave. Once in the car, she prayed traffic would cooperate. *I really messed up this time.*

Jamal stood in the lobby of the Beverly Hills hotel waiting for Asia. He spoke to his colleagues as they passed him on their way to the small ballroom. Dinner would start in ten minutes. *Where is she?* After waiting a few more minutes, he went to take his seat.

Eric looked up when Jamal approached the table. "Is she here?"

He shook his head, took out his phone and sent her a text. Two other couples joined them and Eric introduced Kathi. His gaze strayed to the lone empty chair at the table and the pain in his chest magnified.

One of the senior attorneys came over and shook hands with everyone. "Jamal, where's your lovely wife this evening?"

"She had an emergency at work." Or at least he hoped that was the reason. He would never have missed something so important when it came to her job.

"Well, I hope she makes it."

Jamal pasted what he hoped was a genuine smile on his face. "So do I."

After the man moved on, Kathy caught his gaze and mouthed, "She'll be here."

The waitstaff came around and placed salads and bread on the tables, and filled glasses with water and iced tea.

He picked at the salad and sipped the tea, but he needed something stronger. He excused himself from the table and searched out one of the cash bars set up on either side of the room and ordered his usual whiskey on the rocks. He wanted to toss it back like he was doing shots, but resisted the urge and settled for a long sip. Jamal made his way back to the table, just as someone asked about the class action case.

Eric said, "We're still gathering new information, so it'll be a while before we go to court."

"Unless the owner decides to settle," Jamal added. They'd be meeting with the owners next week and, with the damages stacking up, it might be in the company's best interest.

"Some companies are willing to take their chances with a jury because they think some technicality will get them off with a slap on the wrist."

Eric took a sip of water. "I hope they don't test it."

Jamal agreed. He and Eric were being careful not to miss one thing. The conversation turned to other cases and general subjects from the current political climate to favorite hobbies. All the while, the staff weaved in and out serving each course. Jamal contributed to the conversation and laughed at the appropriate times, but he kept his eyes on the doors watching, waiting. He didn't have an appetite and left more than half of his food on the plate. By the time dessert came, he had all but given up hope that his wife was coming and it broke his heart.

Eric leaned over. "Hang in there. I'm sure Asia has a good reason for being late."

His friends seemed convinced, but the jury was still out in his mind.

The managing partner of the firm stepped up to the microphone. "I hope you all enjoyed dinner. I'd like to thank you all for coming. I know you look forward to attending a gathering that doesn't include assignments." Whistling and shouts of agreement met his statement. He waited until the noise died down before continuing. "This has been a year of continued growth and many triumphs, as well as some rising stars in the firm. First, I'd like to welcome our newest employees." Mr. McCarthy rattled off the names of two associate attorneys, a paralegal and two legal assistants.

Jamal joined the applause, then glanced down at his watch and back over to the door again. He tried to focus on the man's words, but every scenario of why Asia wasn't there ran through his head. Had she been in an accident? Was she somewhere hurt? Or had she simply "canceled" on him again? He didn't want to think it was the latter.

"This year there have been two attorneys who have distinguished themselves with their tenacity and work ethic. I'm proud to announce that Eric Dawson and Jamal Montgomery will be promoted to junior partners."

Before he could finish his statement, the room erupted in cheers. Kathi launched herself at Eric and Jamal felt a touch of jealousy. He and Eric stood and walked to the front to accept the congratulations and marble plaque. When they got back to the table, Kathi was still on her feet clapping. She hugged Jamal.

"I'm so excited for you. Congratulations."

"Thanks, Kathi."

He and Eric shook hands and Eric said, "Senior partner up next."

In spite of his mood, Jamal smiled. "You know it." Everyone around him offered their best wishes. At thirty-five, making junior partner in the large firm was a feat. He was proud of his accomplishments, but the one person with whom he wanted to share his moment never bothered to show up.

Mr. McCarthy announced a few more promotions of those who'd made senior partner. "In closing, I just want to say that this firm is only as successful because of you. Until next year."

All the occupants stood and gave him a rousing applause, then music started. Some people headed to the dance floor, while others decided to call it a night. Jamal stood, intending to leave and saw Asia frantically searching the room. When their eyes locked, she pushed through the throng of people and rushed across the room.

Asia threw her arms around his waist. "Oh, Jamal, I'm so sorry. My boss summoned me to her office right as I was leaving to talk about the housing discrimination piece and she gave me another assignment and was explaining it and I didn't know it was so—"

"We'll talk when we get home," he said quietly. Her words came out so fast, he could barely understand her. With people staring, he didn't want anyone in his business.

She dropped her arms and searched his face. "You don't believe me?"

Jamal wanted to say yes—she looked and sounded sincere—but he didn't know what to think. He obviously hesitated too long because she spun around and started off. He caught her hand. "Asia, I didn't say that."

"You didn't say anything."

The tears standing in her eyes gave him pause. His tough girl rarely cried. He tilted her chin and touched his mouth to hers. "I believe you."

"Asia!" Kathi hurried over and engulfed Asia in a hug. "I'm glad you made it."

"I didn't think I would. Hey, Eric."

Eric bent and kissed Asia's cheek. "Good to see you." He shifted his gaze to Jamal. "Are you guys staying?"

Jamal shook his head. "I think I'll call it a night." Eric and Kathi divided a wary glance between Jamal and Asia. "We're fine. Congrats, again."

"You, too. I think we're going to do the same. See you on Monday." Eric steered Kathi toward the exit.

He gently grasped Asia's hand as they followed. "Did you use the valet?"

"Yes. I was so late, I didn't want to have to bother with parking." She dug the ticket out of her purse and passed it to Jamal.

Outside, he handed the valet both tickets. While waiting, they didn't talk. When the cars were brought around, he helped her in. "I'll be right behind you." In a way, he was glad they had driven separately because he needed to think and prepare himself for the full story. From what he could understand, her boss had called her into the office at the end of the day. Could the meeting have lasted more than an hour? And what was so pressing that couldn't wait until next week? True, he had the occasional last minute meeting at the end of the day, but none that lasted long enough to make him miss an event.

Half an hour later, he parked next to her in the garage and got out. As soon as the side door closed, Jamal said, "Okay, what happened?"

Asia placed her purse on the kitchen table. "Lori asked me to come to her office when I was getting ready to change and leave. I thought it was about the piece I'd written, and it was, for about fifteen minutes."

"You couldn't tell her you had a prior engagement?"

She cut him a look. "Before I could say anything, she handed me a folder with another assignment, this one covering a Carnivale festival in Chicago next month. I was so excited when she started explaining what she wanted me to for the weekend, that I lost track of time. Then there was an accident." She threw up her hands. "Nothing went the way I planned," she said, rubbing her temples. "I know things between us have been strained, but I would *never* intentionally miss something like this."

He folded his arms and leaned against the bar. "I had my doubts. How did we get here?"

"I don't know," she whispered. "And I don't know how to fix it."

Jamal blew out a long breath and pulled her into his arms. "I don't either."

"Will you come with me to Chicago? I know I have to work, but we can spend my free time together. Maybe a change in scenery will help?"

He was all for whatever would restore the closeness they once shared and hoped this trip could be a new beginning. He didn't think he could take the alternative.

CHAPTER 4

*F*riday evening, Asia stuck an earphone in as she rummaged through the refrigerator. "I'm really excited that Lori liked the piece."

"Girl, I knew she would," Dena said. "I can't wait to read it. I'm going to buy copies of the magazine for everybody I know, just so I can say, 'I know her.'"

"Aw, thank you." She pulled out the thawed chicken breasts, bell peppers and an onion. She needed something simple and quick, since it was already six. Asia had made a concerted effort to get home and cook, so she and Jamal could have dinner together. It would be the first time in... She couldn't even remember. Not good.

"You know I'm going to do the same," Marcia chimed in. "But what I really want to talk about is that Chicago assignment. I've been waiting over a week since you sent that text."

"Sorry, it's been busy. It's for something called the Chi-Flavor Afro-Caribbean Carnivale. I'd never heard of it, but I looked it up and it's an annual festival with lots of vendors, music and entertainment, as well as a parade. I'll be doing some interviews and taking pictures."

Marcia squealed. "Ooh, wee! That sounds like fun. We should go with you."

"Actually, Jamal is going with me."

"Does that mean you guys have made up?"

"Dena, I wish it were that simple. Let's just say we're trying." Since the banquet a week ago, they both had made an effort to cut their after work hours. Over the past several months, they'd canceled lunches, dinners, and everything in between. Asia had awakened one day and realized she and Jamal had become virtual strangers.

"I'm glad and I hope you can work out your differences. You and Jamal belong together." Dena chuckled. "The love between you two is so strong, you can feel it."

"Hmm."

"Wait," Marcia said. "Are you saying you don't love him anymore?"

Asia braced her hands on the counter and sighed. "No, I'm not saying that. I love him, but... Oh, I don't know. It's like we're so far apart that sometimes I can't *feel* the love. I don't even know if that makes sense."

"It makes sense, sis. What you and Jamal need is some time away with no interruptions. No cell phones, no jobs, nothing, except the two of you. Use that time in Chicago to your advantage."

That was why she loved Dena. Asia could always count on her for good advice, even if she didn't necessarily care for it. "Remember, I will have to work a good portion of the time."

"But when you're not..."

"Yeah, I know." She would probably have to cover some of the day and night hours, but her friend was right. To save her marriage, she'd make it work. "Thanks for listening. I need to get dinner done before Jamal gets home."

"You know we've got you, girl," Marcia said. "Enjoy that sinfulicious man of yours," she added with a laugh.

Asia shook her head. "I can't with you, girl. Get off my phone." They all laughed.

"*Bye!*" they chorused in singsong.

Still smiling, she disconnected, removed the earphones and placed the phone on the bar. On her way to the counter, she turned on her Bluetooth speaker and cued up one of her playlists. The music kept her company as she diced the vegetables and seasoned the meat. Asia was so focused on humming, dancing and cooking that she nearly dropped the plate holding the now done chicken when she turned from the stove and saw Jamal standing there. "Oh, my goodness! You scared the crap out of me." Her hand went to her chest and she set the plate down while trying to slow her heart rate. "I didn't hear you come in."

A lazy grin tilted the corners of Jamal's mouth. "That's because you were too busy singing and dancing. Smells good." He gestured to the plate.

"Thanks. I thought we could eat together tonight."

Jamal angled his head thoughtfully. "I'd like that. Let me get out of these clothes and I'll be right back."

Asia nodded, or at least she thought she did. His intense stare and the mention of him taking off his clothes brought to mind that they hadn't made love in almost a month. As soon as he was out of sight, she let out the breath she'd been holding. *Maybe this dinner wasn't a good idea.* She pushed the negative thought aside and took the food to the eat-in kitchen table. Along with the chicken, peppers and onion, she added small bowls of cheese and sour cream, and salads for each of them.

"What do you want to drink?"

She spun around at the sound of Jamal's voice. "I made some lemonade."

"Okay." Jamal took down two glasses, tossed in a few ice cubes, and filled them with the sweet drink from a pitcher in the refrigerator. He came over and set a glass in front of each of their place settings.

She jumped slightly when he moved to help her with her chair. "Thanks." He'd always done this, whether they were in public or here at home.

He waited until she assembled her fajita on the tortilla before doing his own. "Is everything set for the Chicago trip?"

"Yes. I got the plane ticket today and I went online and booked yours for the same flight. I wanted to make sure we got seats together."

"I booked my Sunday flight to New York for the afternoon, so that'll give us a few more hours and we can, at least, have breakfast together." Jamal, Eric and two other attorneys were flying to attend a series of meetings related to one of their cases and would return the following Thursday.

"Okay. How's the class action case going?"

"Still getting new information related to medical issues and other tests. I think it's going to get worse."

Asia didn't ask for details because she knew he was bound by confidentiality clauses, but he looked tired. "I hope it doesn't go too long."

"So do I. Tell me about the piece you did on housing discrimination."

She shared her findings and told him about the experiences of the two couples. "I knew it still existed, but I was shocked to learn how just how bad things are, especially with the real estate agents." She made a sound of disgust. She didn't remember them having the same issue when they purchased their Manhattan Beach home shortly after being married. Then again, Jamal had casually let it slip that he was an attorney and had been no nonsense. With him glaring at the agent, the man would have been a fool to try something so ridiculous.

"I'm glad we didn't have the same problem."

"I was just thinking the same. You had that agent scared to do anything other than what we asked, so that helped." They shared a smile.

Jamal finished the last bite of his second fajita. "Whatever works. That was good. Thanks."

Asia picked up a stray pepper and popped it into her mouth. "You're welcome." They continued to converse, talking more about their jobs, Eric and Kathi's pregnancy announcement and everything else. Except themselves. She certainly wanted to proceed with caution. Last week's banquet continued to weigh heavily on her mind, particularly since she had finally learned that he'd been promoted to junior partner. She'd seen the plaque when he placed it on the dresser and it made her feel even worse that she had been so late. Despite the problems plaguing their relationship, she should have been there with him to celebrate and cheer because making *partner* was a big deal.

"Since you cooked, I'll take care of the dishes."

"That works for me." Asia didn't mind cooking, but she hated washing dishes, always had. She stood and took her plate and glass to the sink and Jamal followed. She turned to find him staring at her. "Something wrong?"

"No." Jamal bent and placed a lingering kiss on her lips. "I enjoyed having dinner together."

"Me, too." It wasn't the easygoing kind of conversation like they used to have. Some parts still felt awkward, as if they were afraid of shattering the fragile bond they were trying to rebuild, but it was a start. And she'd take that for now.

～

Jamal sank a jump shot and accepted the ball from Eric. It

had been several weeks since they'd met for a Saturday workout and one-on-one basketball game. The workout helped to relieve a lot of the tension he'd been carrying around from work and home. Eric assumed a defensive stance and Jamal did a spin move, dribbled the ball across the half court and made a layup. "You're getting soft, old man," he teased.

Winded, Eric shot him a glare. "Shut the hell up. You're the same damn age."

He grinned. "Maybe, but I'm not the one wheezing like I'm having an asthma attack." His body let him know it had been a while, but he had no intentions of letting Eric know. Although the gym had air conditioning, somehow, the July heat seeped through and it was enough to make him want to take a dive in the pool.

"Keep talking and you will be." Eric stole the ball and dunked it. "Old, my ass," he muttered.

Jamal bounced the ball to him. "Yeah, your *ass* is old." They kept up the trash-talking until the game ended with Jamal winning by one point. The two men grabbed towels from their individual bags and wiped the sweat from their faces, then sat on the edge of the court drinking bottles of water. "I needed that." His workout regimen had taken a hit over the past month and he'd been lucky to get two days in a week. He thought about converting one of the five bedrooms in his house into a gym. It would save him some money and he wouldn't have to leave his house to drive eight miles to the overpriced athletic club he'd been paying dues to for almost a decade. The older he got, the more he craved convenience.

"How are you and Asia doing?"

He shrugged. "Okay. We've eaten together three times in the past two weeks, but we're still walking on eggshells."

"Have you talked?"

Jamal tilted the bottle to his lips and took a long drink. "Sure. If you mean about our jobs, politics, and stuff on the news, then yeah, we've talked."

Eric stared. "You haven't discussed all the…?" He waved a hand.

"Nope. I think we're both afraid of saying something that might make everything worse, but I don't know how much longer I can deal with things the way they are now." At one point, it had been easier to work late than to come home to an empty house or a silent one. But he'd bitten the bullet and decided it was time to confront things head on. Except he hadn't. Jamal made a living negotiating and arguing, yet, he was tongue-tied when it came to his own issues.

"You're going to Chicago next weekend. That'll be a good time to talk."

"Nah. That's a working trip for her and I'm not going to risk messing it up." If they got into it, she wouldn't be able to do her job well and that's the last thing he wanted. He respected her too much.

"But then, we're heading to New York right after."

Jamal leaned his head against the wall. "I know. It's like we take one step forward and two backward." Last night, he'd come to bed hoping the reestablish some level of intimacy, but Asia had papers covering the bed and her laptop open. The few minutes of work she promised turned into much longer. He'd fallen asleep and woken up two hours later to find her still in the same spot typing. Deciding he needed to change the subject, he asked, "Is the band playing tonight?"

"Two shows."

"I'm going to see if Asia wants to come. We haven't been on a date in months."

"Cool. I'll look for you at either seven or nine-thirty."

"How's the CD coming?"

Eric smiled. "Great. We've laid half of the eleven tracks

and I'm enjoying working with Monte." Terrence "Monte" Campbell was one of the most successful R&B singers and producers in the country. Terrence had come to a show last year as a favor for the husband of Kathi's best friend. Four months later, a contract had been signed and the band would be releasing their first single soon.

"Did you guys settle on a title yet?"

"Passionate Promises. I figured since my baby got me the inside track, I'd honor her by titling the project after the song I wrote for her."

"I expect the first copy," Jamal said, standing. His muscles were starting to cool and he could feel the effects of the intense workout. "Same time, two weeks from now?"

"Definitely. You won't get off so easy next time." Eric started for the exit.

He snorted. "Please. You wish you could keep up." They went their separate ways in the parking lot. "Later."

When Jamal got home, he found Asia putting on her shoes. "Hey. Going somewhere?"

"Hi, and yes. Dena asked me to go shopping with her. Her cousin is getting married and she needs a dress."

"Will you be back early enough to go see Eric's band play tonight? They have two shows, seven and nine-thirty."

Asia stood and eyed him. "It's only three-thirty. Why wouldn't I be back? We're just going for one dress."

"It's shopping and you're women," he said, as if that explained everything.

She rolled her eyes, but smiled. "Whatever. We can go to the seven o'clock show. And if I'm back within two hours, you throw in dinner."

A slow grin tilted the corners of his mouth. "Deal." It was the first time in a while that they'd bantered this way and it gave him hope that they were still going in the right direction. He kissed her.

She drew back and wrinkled her nose. "You smell like you've been playing ball. I sure hope you won."

Jamal playfully swatted her on the behind. "I thought you were going shopping. And, yes, I won."

Chuckling, Asia picked up her purse and strode out.

He shook his head and stripped off his shirt, then frowned. She did have a point. He headed for the shower.

Twenty minutes later, and smelling much better, Jamal loped down the stairs and went to make a sandwich. While eating, he worked on a few documents to get a jump on the upcoming week. Since making junior partner, his workload and responsibilities had increased and he seriously wondered if the promotion had been a good thing. However, in the scope of things, Jamal knew it was because, as he always said, he loved his career choice and couldn't imagine doing anything else. And if he ever decided to step out on his own, he'd have all the tools he needed to ensure his success.

Jamal turned at the sound at the garage door opening. He checked the time. Asia had made it back with eight minutes to spare and the smile on her face said she knew it.

"So, about that dinner. I already know what I want."

"I'm sure you do. We can leave in half an hour."

"Okay."

He watched her departure, then turned his attention back to the document on his screen. He read over what he'd already written and made a few changes before shutting everything down and going to change.

When Jamal and Asia entered the restaurant later, he spotted Eric sitting at the bar. The hostess led them to a table with a reserved sign located in the front at center stage.

"I didn't know you could reserve tables," Asia said.

"I'm sure that's Eric's doing. I'll have to thank him." As soon as the words left his mouth, Eric appeared at the table.

"I'm glad you made it," Eric said. He bent and placed a kiss on Asia's cheek.

Asia smiled. "Thanks for the table. Is Kathi coming tonight?"

"No. She was feeling a little tired, so I told her to stay home."

"I'll have to call her. Other than that, is everything with the baby alright?"

"Yes, she had a few days of mild morning sickness, but that's it."

Jamal couldn't stop the touch of jealousy that surfaced. A family. That's what he wanted with Asia. As if reading his thoughts, Eric placed a reassuring hand on Jamal's shoulder. When the server came to take their order, Eric left to join the band for the warm-up.

Throughout dinner, he and Asia conversed softly, still mostly staying away from any subject surrounding their relationship, but she'd smiled, scooted close to him when the music started and didn't pull away when he'd held her hand. He'd missed this. He'd missed *them*. And he planned to show her how much next weekend when they went to Chicago.

CHAPTER 5

*S*aturday afternoon, Jamal held Asia's hand as they strolled through the festival in *Huntington Bank Pavilion at Northerly Island.* There were all kinds of vendors, games and rides. When they'd arrived yesterday, Asia hadn't done much in the way of working, except talk to a few of the organizers and take some pictures. However, this morning, they'd gotten up for the parade that kicked off at *Soldier Field* and ended at the island. Several bands and dancers had been included and he had watched, fascinated, as his wife worked the crowd. He had never seen her in her element and felt an overwhelming sense of pride. Asia had mentioned there being an opening for a senior writer at the magazine and, from the bit of her housing discrimination piece he'd read, he knew she deserved the promotion.

"This is great! I don't understand how I never knew about this festival, especially since I love this kind of thing. And with it being located along Lake Michigan, the view is gorgeous."

"It is pretty cool."

"The vibe is so infectious I can't help but want to dance."

Asia started moving her shoulders to the music being played by one of the performers that could be heard in the distance. "They said there are about eight thousand people who'll attend *daily*."

Jamal moved closer to her to let a group of people pass. He could believe that. The crowd had grown steadily since the morning and he and Asia had to walk single-file in some places due to the number of people passing. "Is there anything you want to do while you have a few minutes?"

Asia looked up at him. "Eat. I'm starving. I have to interview tonight's headliner in about forty-five minutes, so we should be able to find something before then."

He placed a hand in the small of her back and guided her toward the area holding the food vendors. After several minutes, they decided on a simple burger and fries.

While eating, she asked, "What are you going to do while I'm conducting my interview?"

Jamal shrugged. "Probably wander around a bit and listen to some of the music. Any idea how long the interview will take?"

"No more than an hour, then we can go back to the hotel for a while. I need to be back for tonight's show."

The hotel was only a couple of miles away, so getting back wouldn't be a problem. And with the sun beating down on him, he was all for rest and relaxation in a nice air conditioned room. They finished eating and he escorted her over to where she'd be doing the interview.

Taking Jamal's hand, she introduced him to the band members. "This is my husband, Jamal Montgomery."

Jamal greeted them all. "I'll get out of your way, so you can get started." To Asia, he said, "I'll be back in about forty-five minutes."

"If I'm done before then, I'll wait over there." She pointed to a small group of benches not far away.

He nodded, but didn't immediately leave. Instead, he took up a position not far away and, once again, marveled at her interviewing skills. At one point, she threw her head back and laughed. The sound hit him square in the chest, just as it had done the first time he heard it when he saw her at a café near her job. He couldn't remember why he'd been in the area, but he had stopped to grab some lunch before heading back to the office. She had been sitting with her two friends, Dena and Marcia, and Jamal thought she was the most beautiful woman he had ever encountered with her sparkling dark brown eyes, magnetic smile and sultry voice. She happened to turn in his direction briefly and smile. Her smile had done him in...*instantly*. Before he left, he had boldly introduced himself and asked her if they could meet there for coffee or lunch one day. She accepted and he hadn't looked at another woman since. There had been a good number of women who'd come on to him, but Jamal only had eyes for Asia. Still did. A pang of sadness hit him when he realized that she hadn't laughed for him or been that open and happy in he didn't know how long.

At length, he strolled through the area again, smiling at the exuberance of two children who had won one of the games. His steps slowed when he spotted a booth advertising strawberry shortcake. It was Asia's favorite dessert, and the more whipped cream, the better. An idea popped into his head and a slow grin spread across his face. He'd be back for it before meeting his wife.

Continuing his walk, Jamal stopped to listen to some of the local musical artists and even purchased a CD. On his way back to Asia, he stopped for the dessert and got an extra bowl of whipped cream. When he asked, the vendor graciously provided a bag. Jamal didn't want her to know the contents until they got back to the hotel. She was still talking to the musician and his band when he arrived, so he took a seat on the nearby bench and waited. He was tempted to check his emails, but resisted the urge. He'd be flying out to New York tomorrow for work and that would be soon enough. Jamal couldn't remember the last time he had gone a full day without logging on and it felt good. He decided at that moment he'd make it a practice to forego anything resembling work at least one day of the weekend. A touch on his shoulder brought him back.

"You okay?"

He glanced up to find Asia staring down at him, her eyebrows knitted in concern. He stood. "I'm good. Just thinking. All done for now?"

"Yep. We can head back to the hotel. I want to be back around six-thirty, so I have time to take a few pictures before the show. That'll give me a good two and a half hours to chill." She fanned herself. "And cool off."

"Works for me. We can get an early dinner or wait until after you're done, whichever you prefer," Jamal said as they made their way toward where they had parked the car.

"Can we do it after? I don't want to have to rush."

"Whatever you want, baby."

Asia's gaze flew to his. Their eyes held briefly before she turned away and continued walking.

He guessed she'd paused at the endearment. Something else that had gone by the wayside over the past several months, except during the infrequent times they made love.

"What's in the bag?"

"Just a little something I picked up. I'll show you when we get to the hotel."

"And you can't show me now because?"

"It's a surprise."

She stopped walking. "Seriously? Come on. You've got me curious."

"You'll be alright for the next five or ten minutes."

She stuck out her bottom lip and strutted off ahead of him.

Chuckling, he caught up to her. "You know I'm immune to that pouting." Early in their relationship, all she had to do was give him a sad look and he caved faster than the time it took to blink.

As soon as the door closed to the hotel room, Asia said, "Okay, we're back. What's in the bag?"

Jamal shook his head, retrieved the dessert and a spoon and handed it to her.

Her eyes lit up. "Please tell me this is my favorite strawberry shortcake." She opened the container. "And it has a lot of whipped cream just the way I like. *Yes!*" She plopped down on the small loveseat and quickly dug in. She moaned with the first bite and her eyes slid closed.

He hardened immediately.

"Did you get you one, too?" she asked after half the dessert was gone, eying the bag.

"No." He took out the bowl of whipped cream.

"Aw, you got me extra whipped cream."

"Actually, this is for my dessert."

"They had brownies there?" she asked around a spoonful.

Jamal shook his head slowly. "No, my caramel drop. This is for you. You're my dessert." He saw the moment she understood.

Asia gasped softly.

He gently took the container from her hand, replaced the top and stored it in the small refrigerator. As he walked toward her, he opened the buttons on his short-sleeved shirt one by one, then discarded it. Taking her hand, he pulled her to her feet at the same time his head descended. Unlike the few kisses they'd shared recently, this one was all-consuming. He wanted her to know how much he'd missed being with her this way. He eased back and whipped her shirt over her head, tossing it aside. Jamal retrieved the fluffy cream, and smeared it over her exposed chest. He charted a path with his tongue, not missing one drop.

"I...*ooh.*"

Her knees buckled and he caught her around the waist and backed her toward the bed. "Yeah, I think I'm really going to enjoy my dessert." And he was going to have a hell of a time leaving her tomorrow.

Sunday afternoon, Asia dropped her bags by the front door and sighed in relief. Today had been her favorite day of the festival with the Caribbean and Afro-Caribbean artists performing. There was just something about the lively music and dance that moved her. The trip had been a good one, even more so between her and Jamal, but she was glad to be home. She should probably wash for the upcoming week, but all she wanted to do right now was shower and lay down. The four plus-hour flight had been noneventful and, thankfully, nonstop. No rushing to avoid missed connections, just one straight flight. Leaving the bags there, she trudged up the stairs to the bedroom, found a pair of comfortable leggings and a tee, then headed for the shower.

She felt infinitely better afterwards and wondered if Jamal had made it to New York yet. He left two hours after her flight, but had gone to the airport with her. A smile curved her lips at the memory of the decadent dessert he'd served yesterday. He'd used every drop of that whipped cream on her body and had made her come multiple times. They hadn't made love so passionately in a long time and, unlike the past few times when she'd left the bed immediately after and stayed in the bathroom until he fell asleep, yesterday, she didn't want to leave the bed or him.

Asia went down to the kitchen and made a salad with chopped chicken breast, then sat down to check her emails. She frowned at one from a resort in Jamaica and clicked on it. "Oh, shoot!" She and Jamal had booked the all-inclusive vacation over eighteen months ago through some travel special and it had totally slipped her mind with all they'd been going through. Her hand hovered over the delete button for a few seconds before she decided to wait. The email allowed them to check-in remotely for their Tuesday arrival to bypass the lines at the resort. At this point, she didn't know whether they'd still be able to make the trip, especially since he wasn't supposed to be back until the end of the week, but she would ask when he called tonight. Maybe they could even change the dates to later in the week. The trip would be a good way to continue what they'd started in Chicago.

She sent several other emails to the trash and marked a few others as spam. Her hand stilled when she came across one from someone named Stephanie Carlson. It took her a moment to figure out why the name sounded familiar, then it dawned on her. She was employed as a paralegal at the same firm where Jamal worked and Asia had met the woman on several occasions during events sponsored by the company. But why would she be sending Asia an email and how did she get her address in the first place? Curious, she clicked on it and read: *You can't keep him happy, but I can.* "What the...?" Asia clicked on the attachments and saw photos of Stephanie and Jamal in various places. Together. One in particular of her draped all over Jamal at some tropical beach nearly stopped her heart. She gasped sharply and her fork clattered to the table. Hot tears stung her eyes. *Jamal was cheating on her.* Had this weekend been nothing more than him wanting to eat his cake and have it, too? She pushed her plate away, her appetite now gone.

Asia swiped at the tears that streamed down her face. *Well, he can have all the cake he wants, except mine.* She'd thought they were good, but, obviously, she was wrong. The only thing they were good for now was being done. Completely. She ran upstairs where she had left her phone plugged in and called Dena. As soon as her friend answered, she tearfully told her what happened.

"Oh, no. Are you sure? Maybe it was someone else."

"Dena, I know my husband's body when I see it."

"What did he say?"

"Nothing because he's gone to New York on business." Immediately, an image of Jamal and Stephanie sharing a hotel room filled her mind. Eric had gone on the trip, as well. Was he covering for his friend, or did he even know? "He doesn't get back until Friday, but I'll be gone by then. I'm filing for divorce first thing in the morning."

"Now hold on a minute, Asia," Dena said.

"There's nothing to hold on to. Jamal made sure of that," she added bitterly.

"I'm worried about you. Maybe I should come spend the night with you."

"Can I stay with you, instead? I don't want to spend another moment in this house." Every inch of the space reminded her of him. Of them. Of what no longer would be.

"Sure. Do you want me to pick you up?"

"No, thanks. And it'll only be for a couple of nights."

"What are you going to do after that?"

"I'm going to Jamaica. We were supposed to go together and we booked it so long ago, I'd forgotten about it." She was taking that trip. Alone. Chances were if she had forgotten about it, Jamal had, too, and that was just as well because she needed to get as far away from him as possible.

"Ah...okay. Are you certain this is what you want to do?"

That photo flashed in her head again, accompanied by the

searing pain in her heart. "Yes," she whispered. The tears
started again. "I'll see you in a little while." Asia placed the
phone on the nightstand. Her gaze strayed to their wedding
picture hanging on the wall. She'd been so happy that day.
With her heart shattered into a million pieces, she curled up
on her bed and cried.

Asia didn't know how much time had passed before she
dragged herself up and washed her face. She unpacked the
clothes she'd taken to Chicago and added them to the washer
with the rest of the load. While waiting, she used one suitcase
for the Jamaica trip and would use the other two for most of
her other things. She would have to come back at some point
to pick up her remaining things, but for now she had enough
to last for a while.

Once the clothes were done and she added what she
wanted to the luggage, she loaded them into her car. Asia
scribbled a quick note for Jamal and placed it on top of the
bar. She removed her wedding rings and laid them on top. A
sob escaped her mouth. She took one last look around at the
home she loved, rushed out to her car and backed out of the
driveway. She didn't look back.

As soon as she opened the door, Dena pulled Asia into her
condo and gave her a strong hug. "Come on. We'll get your
bags in a few minutes." She led Asia over to the sofa. "What
do you need me to do for you?"

Giving her a watery smile, she said, "You're already doing
it. Thanks for taking me in."

"You know I've got your back, girl, just like you've always
had mine." Dena's last breakup with an abusive boyfriend
had made her wary of relationships. Asia and Marcia had
helped her escape and gone with her to file the restraining
order. "How long is the Jamaica vacation?"

"A week. I'll call my office to remind them I'll be out."
Once she'd filled out the check-in form, she had remembered

—and her personal calendar confirmed—that she'd already requested and been approved for the leave time.

"Are you hungry?"

Asia shook her head. The thought of food turned her stomach. "I'm going to bring my stuff in." It took the women two trips to get the luggage inside and into Dena's spare bedroom.

"I just can't believe Jamal would do something like this," Dena mumbled. "The way he looks at you would make any woman jealous."

She accessed her emails from her phone and brought up the photo of Jamal and Stephanie on the beach.

"Damn."

"My thoughts exactly." The smiles on their faces and the comfortable way Jamal held the woman let Asia know that hadn't been the first time they'd been together. She closed the attachment because it only magnified the hurt. Asia was strong. She'd get through this. Eventually.

CHAPTER 6

*J*amal ended the call and frowned.

"Still no answer?" Eric asked as they exited the car. He and Eric had just made it to their hotel. Jamal's flight had been delayed over an hour and, instead of landing at six, the plane touched down just before seven, which made it four at home. Plenty of time for Asia to have made it home. Eric's flight had gotten in twenty minutes earlier and he happened to still be waiting for transportation when Jamal made arrived and they decided to split the cost of a car service.

"No. Her plane landed on time and I checked to confirm."

"Maybe she fell asleep."

"She's a light sleeper and hears every little noise." Something wasn't right. He could feel it. He'd been calling her for the past forty-five minutes and she had yet to answer or respond to his texts. They rolled their bags to the registration desk and gave their names.

"Oh, there's a message here for you," the clerk said.

Jamal all but snatched it, hoping it was from Asia. He muttered a curse.

Eric lifted a brow. "What is it? Is Asia okay?"

He passed Eric the message. "The meetings have been canceled."

Eric groaned. "Meaning we flew across the country for nothing." He pulled out his phone and made a call. "Mr. Perez was hospitalized today for chest pain and they're not sure when he'll be released. Rather than waiting to see, they decided to reschedule."

"Just as well. I need to find out what's going on with my wife." They had made love again that morning before going to breakfast and, just like he had predicted, he'd had a difficult time leaving her at the airport. More than anything, Jamal had wanted to go home and continue to put the pieces of their marriage back together. Now he had a chance. He'd also had an opportunity to read the article she had written in its entirety and the surge of pride he'd felt seeing her name in print as the featured selection was something he wouldn't soon forget. He'd planned to take her out to celebrate at the end of the week when he had originally been scheduled to return, but now he didn't have to wait. He checked the time. "I'm going to see if I can find a redeye, rather than spend the night." Truthfully, he was dead on his feet, but the anticipation of seeing Asia outweighed his fatigue.

"I think I'll do the same."

To the clerk, Jamal said, "Our meetings have been canceled. I'd like to see if I can find a flight out tonight before checking in. Will it be a problem to hold the room until I know for sure?"

"It's no problem at all, Mr. Montgomery. We'll hold your room as well, Mr. Dawson."

"Thanks." They moved off to the side, searched flights. "There's one leaving tonight at nine forty-five."

"That's two hours from now. I think we can make it, since the airport is only three miles away."

They called the airline, paid the upgrade fee, and booked the flight. After canceling their hotel reservation, they took a waiting cab back to the airport. On the way, Jamal tried to call Asia again and got her voicemail. "Hey, baby. Give me a call when you get this message. I just wanted to make sure you made it home safely." He pocketed the phone and stared out the window. Something was definitely up.

"Still nothing?"

He shifted his gaze to his friend. "No. Something's not right. I hope she's okay." She *had* to be okay. He could not lose the woman he loved. Once at the airport, their long strides ate up the distance to get through the TSA checkpoint and to the gate. They made it with fifteen minutes to spare. He glanced over at Eric, who'd fallen asleep ten minutes after takeoff. Jamal usually slept on overnight flights, but not tonight. The turmoil swirling in his gut increased the closer he got to home and kept him shifting in his seat the entire time.

When the plane landed, Jamal was so tired he couldn't see straight. On the way out, he stopped at one of the airport's coffee shops and got a large cup. Thankfully, he didn't have to drive. As he and Eric made their way down to the transportation area, he opened his Lyft app and scheduled a ride.

"My ride says four minutes," Eric said.

"So does mine."

"I know you're worried about Asia, but I'm sure she's okay."

"I hope so," he murmured.

Eric's ride arrived first. "Give me a call and let me know what's up."

Jamal nodded. A moment later, his driver pulled up to the curb. He tossed his bag in the back and slid into the seat. As the man navigated through the mess that was LAX and out to the road, Jamal sipped his coffee and tried to stay awake.

After several sips, his stomach reminded him that he hadn't eaten since yesterday early evening.

Jamal nearly jumped out of the car when the driver parked in front of his house. "Thanks." He rolled his bag up the walk and let himself in the front door. He left the suitcase there and went straight to the kitchen and the entrance to the garage. His was the only car inside and his anxiety climbed higher. He walked over to pour out the remainder of the coffee and saw the piece of paper and Asia's wedding rings.

Jamal's heart started pounding. He picked it up and read: *Since I'm obviously not enough for you, I'll get out of your way.* "What the hell does that mean?" Was she leaving him? And why? He snatched up her phone and called again. Again he got her voicemail. He scrubbed an agitated hand down his face. This couldn't be real. Something had happened between the time they parted at the airport and now and he was going to find out what. Jamal made himself a quick breakfast of scrambled eggs and toast, then showered. He probably should get a couple hours of sleep, but he knew he wouldn't be able to rest until he talked to Asia.

He picked up his phone and dialed her office, but hung up before it connected. He stuck his wallet into his jeans pocket, grabbed his keys off the hook. This needed to be done in person. At nine-thirty in the morning, rush-hour traffic should have been cleared, but it wasn't and that added to his anxiety. When he finally made it to her office, he took a deep breath and entered the building.

"Oh, hey. You're Asia's husband."

Jamal whirled around at the sound of a woman's voice. She'd come out of the office he'd just passed. "Yes."

"Jamal, right?"

She obviously knew him, but he couldn't, for the life of

him, remember her. "Yes. I'm sorry I don't remember your name."

"It's Janelle."

"Nice to see you again."

"Same here. Did Asia forget something for her trip to Jamaica?"

Jamaica? "Ah, yes. I'll just grab it from her office and be out so we don't miss the flight."

"Have a good time."

"Thanks." He continued to Asia's office. He should be grateful that Asia's coworker was a talkative person. Apparently she hadn't realized Asia planned the trip without her husband and hadn't batted an eye when he mentioned picking up something from his wife's office. He stood there a moment, trying to remember why the mention of Jamaica sounded so familiar. *Shit!* He'd totally forgotten about the trip they'd planned almost two years ago. He did a quick search of his emails and finally located the travel confirmation. It said they were scheduled to arrive tomorrow.

Jamal rushed out of the office, back to his car and called the resort. He gave the front desk clerk his name. "We have a reservation starting tomorrow and I wanted to confirm."

"Oh, yes, Mr. Montgomery," she said in accented English. "Mrs. Montgomery already completed the online check-in."

"Great. Thank you."

"Have a safe trip and we'll see you tomorrow."

Jamal checked the itinerary and saw that their flight was supposed to arrive in Montego Bay at three in the afternoon. He tapped the phone against his chin, then started the car. He had to call Eric and his boss, and change his flight. Asia had left him without even trying to work things out and he wanted to know why. She was the most beautiful woman he had ever met and the only one who made his heart beat a little faster. The one who stirred his emotions in a way he

couldn't describe. He wanted his wife back. And he was
going after her.

Asia marveled at the beautiful private villa in Ocho Rios,
Jamaica—living area equipped with a kitchenette on one end,
and a luxurious bedroom holding a king-sized four-poster
bed, rich mahogany furniture, en-suite bathroom with
double vanity and large sunken tub. Situated between the
living and sleeping areas was a private courtyard with a
Roman pool and hot tub. It would have made the perfect
romantic escape, except there was nothing romantic about
her escape. Pain settled in her chest.

"Is there anything else you need, ma'am?"

She turned. The all-inclusive resort even came with
personal butler service. "No. Thank you."

He bowed slightly. "Then I will let you get settled."

She nodded. Once the man was gone, Asia placed the tote
she still held on a chair and took another look around the
quaint living area. She ventured over to the verandah where
a table for two had been set. Too bad she wouldn't need it.
"Might as well get settled in." She turned and gasped sharply.
She clapped a hand over her mouth to cut off the scream
bubbling up from her throat when she recognized her
intruder. Jamal. "What are you doing here?"

"This." He held up a piece of paper. "Why else would I be
here?"

"You should have saved yourself a trip."

He tossed the paper on the table and sighed deeply. "We
need to talk, baby."

She stared at the man who she'd loved with all her heart.
"Oh, so now you want to talk. It's a little late for *talking*."

"Asia—"

She pointed a finger his way. "No, Jamal! The time for talking would've been before I had to cancel reservations for our weekend getaway six months ago because something came up at your job and you just couldn't get away. Or when I sat waiting for you in the restaurant last month and you were forty-five minutes late. Or…" The words stuck in her throat. "Or when you made me believe that we were going to be okay last weekend and I found out it was all a lie."

Jamal crossed the room with lightning speed, his hazel eyes flashing in anger. "You want to play the blame game, huh? Fine. Let's talk about our anniversary last year. I cooked your favorite meal, ran you a bubble bath and spread rose petals on our bed. Do you remember what you did? You came home four hours later than you promised and said maybe we could postpone it for another time because you had some interview you had to prepare for. And let's not count—no, wait, maybe we should count—the seven times in the last eight months we were supposed to go out and you canceled." He paused in the middle of his rant, scrubbed a hand down his face and said softly, "Look, we can stand here all day and yell about who didn't show up for what, but that's not why I'm here. You left me a note, Asia, and I have no idea what you're talking about."

A small measure of guilt surfaced. Had she really canceled their lunch dates *seven* times? And why couldn't she remember those rose petals? It was gone just as fast when she remembered the picture. "I said everything I'm going to say and I've filed for divorce."

"Divorce? I'm not signing any divorce papers. You owe me an explanation."

Her anger spiked. "I owe *you*?! I don't owe you anything. I'm not the one who screwed up our marriage." Asia took a steadying breath. "As I said, there's nothing left to talk about.

All I need from you is to sign those papers and leave me alone."

Jamal's mouth curved in a slight smile and he leaned close enough for their breaths to mingle. "Sorry, my caramel drop, it's not happening."

Asia's breath hitched. Just the mention of her nickname flowing from his honeyed voice brought sensations from the trip to Chicago to life. Annoyed with her reaction, she stormed past him, skirted the pool in the courtyard and entered the bedroom. She felt his gaze on her back, but she didn't turn around. She paced for several minutes. What happened to him getting back from his business trip at the end of the week? Her husband's surprise visit had thrown her for a loop. Even more surprising was her response to him.

Asia paced the stunning bedroom for a good twenty minutes and debated whether or not she should leave. Dropping down on the bed, she heaved a deep sigh. The bed had to be the most comfortable one she'd ever laid on, but one she shouldn't plan on sleeping in. No. They'd already paid for the week. If anyone needed to leave, it was Jamal. "*That's* probably not going to happen," she muttered. Now what? The suite only had one bed and she refused to give it up. She stood and ventured into the bathroom. A Jacuzzi large enough for two people stood in the middle of the floor bordered by candles waiting to be lit. His and hers sinks were situated across from the tub on either side of the room. She groaned. Every inch of the private villa had romance stamped all over it. But, it didn't matter. The damage to their relationship couldn't be fixed.

She heard the sound of water and went back to the bedroom. As she got closer, she realized Jamal was swimming in the small private pool. Asia tried to ignore the way his muscles flexed with each stroke. Her chocolate kiss.

That's what she'd always called him. A tingling sensation started in her midsection, flared out to her breasts and settled between her legs. She closed her eyes as memories of running her hands all over his body and him doing the same to her flooded her mind. Images of his strong body and gentle touch were so vivid she could almost feel his caresses, feel his body against hers. No other man could arouse her the way Jamal could. Asia's eyes snapped open. It took her a moment to notice she didn't hear movement in the water. She edged closer to the sliding glass door and froze. Jamal climbed out of the pool wearing...nothing. She groaned. Maybe she should be the one to leave, or at least see if the resort had something else available. There was no way they could stay in the same room.

CHAPTER 7

*A*sia continued to watch Jamal. Water ran down his smooth brown skin making him look like a black Adonis. Her eyes were glued to every movement he made. As if sensing her presence, he turned and smiled.

"See something you like, Mrs. Montgomery?"

She snatched her gaze from his magnificent physique and tilted her chin defiantly. "Nothing at all," she lied. "And don't call me that." She might be mad as hell at him, but it didn't change the fact that every inch of his body turned her on.

He angled his head thoughtfully and studied her. "You used to like it. What changed?"

Asia couldn't tell him the truth, at least not yet. Parts of her wanted to scream at him and demand that he tell her why he didn't love her. To explain why she wasn't enough and why he needed to sleep with another woman. They would have to talk soon, but right now she didn't trust herself to stay in control. She wanted to throw one of those loungers at his head and that wouldn't be a good idea. Instead she said, "I'm going for a walk." She strolled across the courtyard, determined not to let him see how much he still affected her. As she came closer to where he stood dripping wet, her pulse spiked. *I'm not going to look*, she mentally chanted and dared her eyes to turn his way. He reached out and grabbed her when she passed. Asia sucked in a sharp breath. "What…what are you doing?" she asked breathlessly.

He wrapped his arms around her and pulled her flush against his hard body. "You said things have changed and that I didn't think you were enough. I intend to prove they haven't and you're more than enough for me."

"Let me go, Jamal. You're getting my clothes wet."

"You never minded before. In fact, I seem to recall your favorite solution—getting naked, too."

He pressed his body closer and trailed kisses along her jaw and ear, forcing her to remember just how it felt to have him touch and kiss her. And how good they were together. But she wanted and needed more than just sex and she couldn't forget the fact that he'd betrayed her.

"Do you remember?"

She pushed against his chest and backed out of his hold. "It doesn't matter." This time he released her. She hurried through the yard to the living area.

"Asia?"

She stopped, but didn't turn around.

"We still need to talk."

Without responding, she slid the glass door open, entered the room and closed it behind her with shaky hands. Asia probably should have gone back to change—the front of her sundress was nearly soaked—but she needed to get away from Jamal before she gave in to what her body wanted. She snatched up the card key and her sunglasses, then left the suite. The closer she came to the beach, the calmer she became. Asia slipped off her sandals and let her feet sink into the warm, pristine sand. She sauntered toward the water and noticed she was the only one walking alone. Amorous couples lay cuddled on blankets or strolled hand-in-hand along the shore, while others splashed playfully in the water. Pangs of envy hit her.

She dropped down on the sand and folded her legs beneath her. Jamal accused her of putting her job before their marriage, but he knew she had been working hard to secure a senior writer position and had been supportive at the beginning. She thought he understood that she needed to work longer hours and chase down stories. When they first married, both were working their way up—he at the law firm and she at the magazine—and expected there would be some late hours, but she and Jamal had promised to always make each other the priority and have dinner together as many nights as possible. Somehow, over the last year, sharing meals had diminished and cuddling in bed became nonexistent, aside from the past weekend. Those were the things she missed the most. The question she needed to ask herself was *had she done all those things he accused her of?*

Asia frowned, thinking back to the email and attached photos she had received, the one which prompted her to file for divorce. Although things were bad, not once had she ever thought about going out with another man, not while still married. Apparently, her husband hadn't shared the same sentiment. What she couldn't understand was why he said he'd refuse to sign the divorce papers when he already had someone else waiting. A tingling started down her spine and a shadow fell over her. She didn't have to turn around to know her husband was next to her. Her body never failed to react when he came near.

"It's really beautiful here," Jamal said.

"Yes, it is."

He lowered himself next to her. "It's a perfect spot for lovers."

She slowly faced him and narrowed her gaze. "How

would you know? Did you have someone in mind?" Asia couldn't hide her anger at the thought that he might have brought Stephanie to this place or somewhere similar.

His brows knitted in confusion. "What's that supposed to mean?"

"You know exactly what I mean. Don't try to pretend otherwise."

"I *don't* know what you're talking about, Asia."

"No?" She jumped to her feet. "Well, why don't you ask *Stephanie?*"

He came to his feet swiftly. "What does she have to with us?"

"According to her...*everything!*"

"There is nothing going on between me and Stephanie," he gritted out. "And I don't know why she would say there is."

"That's not what those pictures say," she snapped, pointing her finger in Jamal's face. It should have bothered Asia that they were engaged in a full-fledged argument now and people around them stopped to watch, but at this moment she could care less. *So much for staying in control.*

"Pictures? *What pictures?*"

She pulled her cell from the small pocket on her dress, brought up the photos and thrust the phone in his face. "These!" Jamal took the phone. A myriad of expressions crossed his face—confusion, shock, anger—but not the one she'd expected. Guilt.

"What the hell?" he whispered.

"So, now you're going to tell me that's not you in those photos."

"I wouldn't insult your intelligence, Asia. But, I have no idea how she got these pictures because I've never taken her anywhere near a beach and I definitely didn't pose for any photos with her."

Asia folded her arms. "*Riiight*. So now you're going to tell me you've never gone out with her?"

His jaw tightened. "Asia—"

"That's what I thought." She choked back tears, not wanting to believe he had betrayed her.

He reached for her. "Listen to me."

She slapped his hand away. "No! Don't touch me. I'm leaving." Not giving him a chance to say anything else, she grabbed her shoes and ran as fast as she could with her feet sinking into the sand.

Jamal stared after Asia, his teeth grinding against the others and his jaw so tight he would probably have permanent damage. He noticed several people still watching. The men all nodded sympathetically, while the women glared. He read Stephanie's email again and couldn't believe that she'd had the gall to send Asia this crap. And to insinuate that she'd be able to keep him happy... His rage spiked again. Turning around again, he caught a glimpse of Asia before she disappeared down the path leading back to their suite. He started to follow her, but he was too angry. Angry that Stephanie had fabricated lies and doctored some photos, angry that his marriage had disintegrated to the point that his wife no longer trusted him and angry that Asia was hurting. He wished he could just say forget it and walk away, but he couldn't. They were meant to be together and he wasn't going to allow this to tear them apart. From the day their gazes had first locked in that café, he knew he was destined to love her and he refused to give her up without a fight.

He glanced down at the picture on the screen again and shook his head. Stephanie Carlson was a piece of work. They had gone out twice for drinks before he and Asia met, but once he and his wife got together, he'd made it crystal clear they would be nothing more than colleagues. Or so he thought. The paralegal seemed to sense trouble—he wouldn't put it past her to have been eavesdropping outside his office door—and had come on to him for the past several weeks, but he swiftly and firmly shut her down. The last time had been that night at *Infuse Rhythm Lounge*. Since then, she'd kept her distance, so he figured she'd finally gotten the message. Using his pad of his thumb, he swiped the screen. His eyes widened and his heart nearly stopped upon seeing the image of him reclined shirtless on a lounger with Stephanie draped all over him. "How had she...?" He trailed off, knowing that anything was possible with technology. The longer he stared at the picture, the angrier he got. Jamal remembered exactly where the picture was taken. He sent the email to his phone, typed a short message to Eric and hit the forward button. He sent a second one, more professionally written, to Mr. McCarthy detailing the harassment of his wife and the stress it had caused them both.

A few minutes later, an email from Eric popped up: *You have got to be kidding me. I can't believe she sent this to Asia. I hope you're sending a copy to McCarthy. If you don't, I will.*

Jamal let Eric know that it was already done. He hoped Stephanie had a back-up plan for her career because when he was finished with her, she was going to need one. Right now though, he needed to talk to Asia. Pushing to his feet, he dusted the sand off his shorts and started back to their villa.

The sight of his wife sitting at the edge of the pool with her dress hiked up to her thighs stopped Jamal in his tracks and sent a jolt directly to his groin. His hands itched with the memory of how it felt to trail his hands along her silky skin. One evening in particular stood out in his mind. He had been sitting at their kitchen table preparing for a case when Asia came in and sat on the table. She slid her bare leg up and down his arm and across his chest before straddling him in the chair. Papers and clothes went flying as she took control and drove him to the point of sheer ecstasy again and again. He couldn't ever remember a time when he'd come so hard. They'd nearly toppled the chair over in the process. No other woman could make him lose control and bring him pleasure the way she did. No one.

Dragging his mind back to the present, Jamal slowly approached, kicked off his sandals and sat next to her. For the first few minutes he didn't speak, just watched her swirl her feet in the water.

Finally, he said, "I'm sorry."

She jerked her head in his direction. "I knew it!"

She started to get up and he placed a staying hand on her arm. "Asia, I did not see Stephanie or any another woman behind your back."

Asia snatched away from his grasp. "You just said you're sorry."

"I am. I'm sorry I allowed our marriage to get so bad that you don't trust me anymore. I promise you I've never cheated on you, sweetheart. I don't want another woman," he said with a frustrated sigh. "I just want my wife back." She studied him for a lengthy moment then went back to staring at the water. At least she hadn't stormed off like earlier. He plowed on. "I went out for drinks with Stephanie twice six months before I met you. Maybe I should have told you, but it was completely casual. Nothing more than coworkers hanging out for a few minutes after work. She wanted more and I didn't. I made that clear *then*. And since I met you four years ago, I haven't looked at another woman."

"Why didn't you tell me?"

He shrugged. "I don't know. Again, it happened before we met and it didn't matter. You never mentioned all the guys you dated before we met, either."

"Then how did she get the pictures of you and her together?"

Jamal pulled out Asia's phone and brought up the picture of him shirtless and handed it to her.

She glowered at him. "I don't need any reminders of you with that woman."

He threw up his hand. "Asia, will you just look at the picture? Look closely at the bottom left side and tell me what you see."

She reluctantly took the phone and looked at the picture. "All I see is that trifling ass—"

"Asia, please. Just look."

Asia enlarged the picture and he saw the moment she zeroed in on what he had seen. "Is that...oh, my goodness. *Oh, hell no!* I know she didn't." Her gaze met his. "That's my gold sandal," she whispered in disbelief. "This picture is..." She trailed off and focused on the photo again.

"Yeah, from our honeymoon. The one where we had one of the staff take our picture when we were lounging on the beach. That picture is the screensaver on my work computer."

"You mean she took that picture and edited it?"

"Yes." Asia was already mad, but if he had any hope of restoring his marriage he knew he had to be honest and plowed on. "Stephanie overheard us arguing over the phone the last time you canceled lunch and she tried coming onto me. I shut her down completely and thought that was the end of it."

"I guess not. I don't know what to say." She twisted her hand in her dress. "What are you going to do?"

"I've already done it. I don't want to talk about her anymore. I want to talk about us. How did we get here? We used to have so much fun together. We used to love each other unconditionally. We *trusted* each other."

Asia swiped at the tears on her face and sniffed. "I don't know. It just seems like I woke up one day and we weren't in love anymore."

Jamal reached for her hand and was grateful when she didn't pull away. "I never stopped loving you, Asia. Are you saying you don't love me anymore?" His heart pounded as waited for her answer.

"I honestly don't know. There's just so much stuff going on inside me and—"

He released her hand, feeling as if a knife had been plunged into his heart. It never crossed his mind that she might not love him anymore. "I see. I guess the promise we made to each other the day we married didn't mean as much to you as it did to me." He stood and walked to the bedroom. He always thought they would be able to work through any obstacle. But, for the first time, he started to wonder if the marriage would survive, after all.

CHAPTER 8

*A*sia stared after Jamal's retreating back, her heart breaking. His stricken expression would forever be etched in her mind. She dropped her head in her hands. She hadn't meant to hurt him, but she seriously thought he'd been having an affair all this time. The tears started again. Why had she been so quick to believe a lie and what kind of a woman would stoop so low as to send doctored photos? Deep down inside she knew lying and cheating wasn't part of his DNA. Whenever he walked into a room, she noticed all the women smiling his way, but from the moment they started dating, he'd only had eyes for her. Then he would give her that smile—the one meant only for the two of them —and her entire body would come alive. She missed the way they could communicate without speaking. But, lately, they hadn't been communicating at all, and she was partly to blame.

Jamal was right. Somewhere along the line she had forgotten their promise—to always talk about everything and to never let go of the love they had built. Asia told him she didn't know if she still loved him, but she'd lied. She had never stopped loving him. And, in just a few short hours, now questioned whether she wanted a divorce at all.

"Excuse me, ma'am."

Asia jumped slightly, but relaxed upon seeing the butler. "Oh, hello."

"I just wanted to let you know your dinner will be served in fifteen minutes. I'll set the table."

She frowned. "I didn't order dinner yet."

"No, ma'am. Your husband did. He asked that a special meal be prepared for you." He bowed slightly and departed.

A special meal? That was just like Jamal. Her curiosity got the best of her. Since he took the time to have a meal prepared, she could at least eat it. And invite him to share it. She sighed. Rising to her feet, she made her way to the bedroom. He lay stretched out on the bed with one arm across his midsection and the other thrown across his face.

"Jamal?"

He slowly drew his arm down and rolled his head in her direction.

"Um...they're bringing dinner in a few minutes. I'm sure you're probably hungry. And, thank you," she added softly. Asia wanted to say so much more, but the words wouldn't come.

Jamal pulled himself to a sitting position. "Are you sure?"

She nodded, turned and walked away. Asia sat in the courtyard observing the staff positioning items on the table. Minutes later, the butler came out to let her know dinner was ready.

"I hope everything is to your liking."

The center of the table held a bouquet of red roses with a single pink one in the center—Jamal's signature bouquet. Her emotions bubbled once more. She tentatively reached for the silver dome at one of the place settings but halted when she heard the butler's voice.

"Good evening, sir. We made sure to prepare the meal to your specifications."

"I appreciate that," Jamal said, coming to stand next to Asia. He pulled out the nearest chair and gestured her to it.

Asia didn't know if it was the spell of the island, the romantic candlelit atmosphere or what, but despite things being unsettled between them, Jamal's nearness stirred the familiar feelings within her that only he could. She sat. "Thank you."

He rounded the table and took the seat across from her. "I hope you like your dinner, Asia."

Asia didn't know what to say. They'd only sat down to eat together a handful of times recently, not counting Chicago. Each encounter seemed forced, not filled with their usual playfulness and laughter. That was something else she'd missed.

The butler lifted the dome. "Lobster medallions in a champagne sauce, steamed asparagus and a baked potato with the works—butter, sour cream, cheese, chives and extra bacon, correct?"

She stole a quick glance at Jamal before answering. "Yes, thank you." Tears stung her eyes. This was the very first meal Jamal had prepared for her after they'd married. He had been so excited about cooking and wouldn't let her in the kitchen. Asia remembered being surprised at how well he cooked and it became her number one requested meal. Memories of them cooking together bombarded her mind. Next, the man picked up the chilled bottle of champagne. She caught a glimpse of the label. It was her favorite, *Moët & Chandon Rosé*. He filled their glasses, bowed and departed. She smoothed the napkin in her lap, feeling a bit nervous and unsure. He had gone to such lengths to make this a special dinner despite the fact that she had left him with nothing more than a note and plans to divorce him. "Why?"

"Why what?"

She waved her hand over the table. "All this."

"I've missed us being together, eating and talking about us, our hopes and dreams. I was hoping you missed it too." Jamal leaned back in his chair and released a long breath. "But that was before our last conversation."

Asia knew he meant her confession of not knowing whether she loved him. "I'm sorry."

"So am I."

She stabbed at the asparagus on her plate then put her fork down. "I...I do love you, Jamal. With all that's happened over the last several months and thinking you were having an affair, I think I just buried those feelings. But they're still there."

He leaned forward and covered her hand with his. "I don't want to lose you, baby. Can we talk, I mean *really* talk and see if we can find our way back?"

Hope sprang in her heart. "I'd like that."

Jamal lifted his glass. "To starting over...and never letting go."

Asia touched her glass to his and repeated his words. "Who's going first?"

"Eat your food, sweetheart. We have all night."

She nodded, picked up her fork again and ate a bite of the lobster. "It's good," she said with a smile.

He returned her smile. "I had to do some serious negotiating to get this meal. Apparently, the chef doesn't like to go off menu, but I was very convincing."

They ate in companionable silence for a few minutes before Asia said, "I'm sorry I wasn't there for you when you received the commendation and promotion to junior partner from your firm. If I had known you were getting it..." Maybe she would have told her boss she had to leave and asked if they could continue their conversation at the start of the week. Whatever way the words came out, the result would have been her leaving *on time*.

"I didn't know for sure and, yes, I was disappointed that the one person I wanted to share my accomplishment with wasn't there until the end. But that's water under the bridge now."

"I promise I won't miss another one. But I need you to be supportive of my work, too."

"Asia, I do support you and I'm very proud of your work and I'm sorry you thought otherwise. The piece you did on housing discrimination was brilliant."

Her eyes widened. "You read it?"

"Yes, and I wanted to celebrate with you, but, when I got home yesterday, you weren't there. And truthfully, I started to feel like your work was becoming more important than us, especially in the last few months."

"Why didn't you tell me?"

"I tried. But I couldn't get five minutes of your time. There were nights when I came home and wanted to make love to my wife and could barely get into bed with all the papers strewn across it while you were buried behind the laptop. We weren't eating together, talking, or doing anything that married couples do. Then I started doing the same thing. At some point, it became easier to stay at work. But I was wrong. I should have fought harder for us. I should've kept making us the priority." He placed his fork on the plate and leaned back in the chair. "I thought we were on our way back after Chicago," Jamal said quietly.

"I should've made us the priority, too. And then I got the pictures." Another wave of guilt surfaced. "We really messed up. We used to always make time for each other and talk about whatever bothered us."

He took a sip of his champagne. "Yeah, we did."

"So, what do we do now?" She didn't want to lose him.

"That depends on you. I want to try to rebuild our marriage, but it'll only work if it's what you want, too."

"I do." She reached for and squeezed his hand.

"Then, this week, no law cases, no magazine articles, or emails. Just you. Just me."

Asia nodded as a tear slid down her cheek. "Just you. Just me." They were going to make it.

Jamal lifted Asia's hand and brought it to his lips, and felt the vise around his heart loosen. "I'm so glad you said that." He picked up his fork and continued to eat.

"By the way, how did you get here before me and what happened to you being in New York for the week?"

"There was a message waiting for us at the hotel letting us know the man we were meeting with had been hospitalized with chest pains, so they canceled the meetings. Eric and I were lucky enough to get a redeye out that night and I got home yesterday morning."

"And then you hopped on another flight to get here. Did you even sleep?"

"Barely. When you didn't return my calls and I found the note, I was desperate. I drove to your office to see if you were there and happened to see one of your coworkers, Janelle."

Asia smiled. "She's pretty cool."

"She is. She asked me if you'd forgotten something for your trip to Jamaica. That's how I figured out where you were." He might have to send Janelle a gift for sharing that piece of information. "Then I remembered the trip and found the email. I changed my flight to get here early because I wanted, no *needed* to know why you'd left me."

"My heart was so broken when I thought you—" She

cleared her throat. "I couldn't say anything. I just needed to get away."

Jamal came and hunkered down next to her. "Know this. I will never love another woman. You are my one and only. *For always.*"

She leaned down and kissed him. "And you're mine."

He placed his forehead against hers. "We're going to be okay."

"Yes, we are, baby."

They shared a smile and he returned to his seat. After dinner, he convinced her to take another walk on the beach. The moon shone brightly in the dark sky, stars twinkled like diamonds and a warm breeze enveloped them.

"I hope we don't see the same people who were out here earlier," Asia said as they strolled hand-in-hand at the water's edge. "Those people probably think we're crazy."

Jamal laughed. "Actually, I was kind of hoping we'd run into them. After you left me, I got some hostile looks from the women."

Asia wrapped her arms around his waist. "I'm sorry about that."

"I'm just happy to have you in my arms again." He stopped walking, pulled her into his embrace and lowered his head. He groaned at the first touch of their lips. It had been too long since they had kissed like this and he needed her like he needed to breathe. With everything in the open, they were free to explore and recapture the essence of their love. Their tongues danced slowly, sensually and he pressed closer, deepening the kiss. They stood under the moonlight kissing as the water lapped their ankles. Finally, Jamal lifted his head.

She smiled. "I missed kissing you like this."

"And I missed kissing you, sweetheart." He gestured her forward and they walked a little further before retracing their steps back to the suite.

Asia came up on tiptoe and placed a quick kiss on his lips. "I'm going to take a shower."

Jamal nodded, watching the sweet sway of her hips until she disappeared into the bathroom. He smiled and his heart did, too.

Asia glanced around the bedroom at her handiwork and smiled.

"I see you were busy while I showered."

She whirled around when she heard Jamal's voice behind her. Her mouth ran dry and her body heated instantly at the sight of him wearing nothing but a towel. A few drops of moisture still clung to his muscled frame and she was tempted to lick them off. The warmth that began in her belly, flared out to every part of her body and settled in her core. "I...um, I guess so." She had lit scented candles and placed them around the room and turned the lamp down to its lowest setting while he showered. "Since you took care of dinner, I thought I'd see to dessert."

Jamal's brow lifted. "Oh? And what's on the menu?"

She walked to where he stood. "Well, more champagne, strawberries with chocolate for dipping and..." She undid the belt of her short robe and let it drop to the floor. "Me."

Desire lit in his eyes. "You remember what happened the last time you brought strawberries and chocolate to bed?"

"With exceptional clarity," she said with a sultry wink.

A wicked grin covered his mouth. "In that case..." He whipped his towel off, swept her off her feet, laid her on the bed then stretched out beside her. "We can save the champagne and I definitely want those strawberries later, but right now, I just want you."

He crushed his mouth against hers in a seductive kiss that

stole her breath. His hands skimmed over her body from shoulder to her hip, electrifying her in the process. Jamal brought one hand up, gently kneading and stroking her aching breasts. He left her mouth, bent his head and captured a hardened nipple between his lips. Asia couldn't stop the moans spilling from her throat. How had she gone without this for so long? His touch. His kiss. He transferred his attention to the other breast while his hand traveled down past her belly and settled between her legs. Her hips flew off the bed when he began stroking her clit in slow, insistent circles.

"You know what?" he murmured. "On second thought, I think I need a little of that chocolate. It's the perfect accompaniment to all this luscious caramel." Jamal reached for the bowl of melted chocolate, painted some on her breasts and made a path down the front of her body. "Now, for the taste test." He slowly and meticulously licked off every drop of chocolate. "Mmm, so good."

Asia thought she might go insane from pure ecstasy. At the first touch of his tongue on her already wet center, she came in a wild rush of pleasure. His tongue delved deeper inside of her, intensifying the sensations and leaving her gasping for breath. Before she could recover, he slid up her body and eased his hard shaft inside until he was buried deep.

He shuddered above her, tipped his head back and closed his eyes. "Asia," he whispered, almost like a prayer.

She ran her hands over the strong, muscular planes of his chest, savoring the feeling of being connected to him in this way again.

Framing her face with his hands, he stared intently into her eyes. "I love you."

"And I love you, Jamal. I'm never letting you go."

Relief washed over his face. "I'm never letting you go. Ever." Jamal lowered his head and kissed her tenderly, reaffirming their promise. He started a slow rhythm, thrusting with long, languid strokes.

Asia called out his name, wrapped her legs around his waist and arched up to meet each deep thrust. Gradually, he increased the pace. Their passionate cries and labored breathing echoed throughout the space. He locked his mouth on hers, his tongue imitating the movements of his lower body. Just like always, he knew what that did to her. Suddenly, her whole body was shaking. She wrenched her mouth away and screamed as she came, racked by uncontrollable, shuddering contractions.

Moments later, Jamal went rigid against her. He threw his head back and released with a loud groan. "You are my life, Asia," he murmured, placing a gentle kiss on her lips. He collapsed on top of her briefly then rolled to his side and took her with him.

She drifted off with a smile on her face.

Asia woke up the next morning, propped on an elbow and watched Jamal sleep. The emptiness in her life was now gone. Nothing else mattered if she didn't have him by her side. She lightly traced the lines on his handsome face and pressed a kiss to his lips. His eyes fluttered then opened. He smiled and her pulse skipped. She snuggled closer to him. "Mmm, morning."

Jamal kissed the top of her head. "Morning, baby."

"I wish we could stay like this forever."

He chuckled. "We can, if you like. We'll just have to do it in our bed. But, maybe we can come back in a few months."

Her head popped up and she said, excitedly, "Really?"

"Really. No more canceling vacations, dinners, lunches. Deal?"

"Deal. But, what if we have to work late? You know both of our jobs require overtime." She didn't want them to fall back into the same habits again.

"True, but we need to limit those times, as well as how much time we spend working at home. I know I'm bad about that."

Asia nodded. "So am I. What if we make a pact to have dinner together, then work for a couple of hours? Make nine-thirty or ten the cut-off time. Afterward, will be our time."

"I can live with that. There's one more thing." Jamal rolled over and swung his legs over the side of the bed.

"Where are you going?"

He walked over to his bag and took out a small jeweler's box. Climbing back onto the bed, he opened the lid, took out the ring and slid it onto her finger. "Let's put this back where it belongs."

"Yes." Asia threw her arms around his neck and covered his mouth in a passionate kiss. She felt his growing erection against her thigh and heard him groan when their mouths made contact. He drew her down to the bed and into his arms. As he thrust deep inside her, she knew he would be all she ever needed.

CHAPTER 9

"*S*o are you going to sit there and daydream or get some work done? I want to get out of here close to on time today."

Jamal frowned at Eric. "I am working."

"No, you're thinking about your wife and all the fun you had in Jamaica," Eric countered.

Jamal smiled, remembering a time when he'd accused Eric of doing the same thing. Except, Eric had been kissing Kathi at *Infuse Rhythm Lounge*, not in a private villa in Jamaica. "Yeah, well, what can I say? We had a good time." A *really* good time after that first day. Two weeks ago, they had been reluctant to leave their rediscovered paradise, and now that they were home, Jamal couldn't be happier about the progress he and Asia had made in that time.

"I'm glad. I hated seeing you both so miserable."

"I was way past miserable," Jamal said with a laugh. It had been the worst time in his life since losing his father at age nineteen. When his hero died of a stroke, Jamal never thought his world would be right again. He knew Eric understood because Eric had lost his parents in an accident when he was twelve. Jamal still had his mother and he made a mental note to call her. She was happily remarried and living in Seattle. "But we're good now." He scooted his chair closer to the conference table and picked up a document. "Which is why I will be out of this office in the next thirty minutes."

Eric chuckled. "That's what I thought."

They finished the notes on a new case involving fraud and called it a day.

On the way to the parking garage, Eric asked, "How do you like the new paralegal?"

"She's smart and all business."

"And that makes our jobs much easier, in and *out* of the office."

"No lie." Eric had sent Jamal an email while he and Asia were still in Jamaica letting him know that Stephanie had been fired. "I'm just glad I don't have to deal with Stephanie anymore."

"She was pissed after her meeting with McCarthy, talking about discrimination, harassment and a whole lot of other mess. But there was nothing she could do when he showed her that email."

Jamal shook his head and got mad all over again. "She's lucky I was in another country when I saw it, otherwise, she might be doing some jail time. She not only harassed my wife, but she went into my office and stole pictures off my computer and doctored them."

Eric clapped Jamal on the shoulder. "Well, it's over now, and you and Asia can get on with your lives. If you're not busy tomorrow night, let's do dinner. Kathi's been bugging me about us doing a double date."

"I'll check with Asia and let you know tonight." He tossed his briefcase in the backseat and slid behind the wheel.

Because the law firm was only a short commute, he made it home first and started dinner.

Jamal was in the middle of seasoning the steaks when he heard the side door open.

"Dang it! I was trying to beat you home today," Asia said, breezing into the kitchen with a huge smile on her face.

He laughed. *This* was how their home was supposed to be. "I just got here ten minutes ago."

She came up on tiptoe and kissed him. "What's for dinner?"

"Steak, roasted potatoes and sautéed broccoli and mushrooms."

"Mmm, sounds heavenly. Let me put this stuff down and I'll do the vegetables. Your steaks are always better, so you get to do that."

"And afterward, I'm going to do you."

Asia gave him a coy smile. "Oh? Why wait until after?" She tossed him a wink and strutted out of the kitchen.

Jamal glanced down at the steak and seasonings lining the counter, then back to the space his wife had vacated. He chose his wife.

Two hours later, they sat down to dinner. "You really need to learn to control yourself," Asia said, forking up a bite of potatoes.

"Me? I'm not the one talking about why wait. I just took you up on your offer." They didn't even make it to the bedroom. He had taken her from behind halfway up the stairs and then again against the wall in the hallway.

She shrugged. "Well, when it's good..." She wiggled her eyebrows and cut into her steak.

"Asia, if you want to finish dinner, you need to stop playing. Otherwise, *I'm* going to be the only one eating." Her mouth formed a perfect O and he burst out laughing.

She mimicked zipping her lips and continued to eat.

Shaking his head, Jamal did the same. "Eric and Kathi want to know if we're available to go out to dinner tomorrow."

"That'll be fine and nice way to end the workweek. Now, guess what?" She smiled and her eyes sparkled.

Jamal paused with his glass halfway to his mouth. "What?" he asked warily.

"You're looking at the new *senior writer* for *Divine Living & Travel* magazine."

"Are you *kidding* me?" He jumped up, pulled her out of her chair and swung her around. "Congratulations, baby. I'm so proud of you." He kissed her. "We have to celebrate."

Laughing, she said, "We already did. I had planned to tell you when I first got home, but you distracted me."

He joined in her laughter. "Guilty as charged. And I'll happily do it again." He figured they could make tomorrow's dinner a celebration of her promotion and Eric and Kathi's upcoming baby, since they had never gotten around to it. Jamal placed Asia on her feet and they finished the meal.

They spent the rest of the evening laughing and talking about what her new position would entail and how his responsibilities had changed. And just like every night since returning from Ocho Rios, she'd slept in his arms.

The next morning, they were almost late for work because Asia had given him a very sensual awakening. As Jamal worked through the day, he found it difficult to concentrate because his mind kept going back to the way she had slid her tongue over his engorged length and every part of his body. His eyes had rolled so far back in his head, it was a wonder he could see straight. His groin stirred and he could feel himself growing hard. His cell buzzed, drawing him out of his lustful thoughts. He clicked on the text from Asia: *I think I need a little more of my chocolate kiss. Maybe I can come to your office at lunchtime. I promise to make it worth your time. A little lick here, there...*

Her words made him even harder and he sucked in a sharp breath. He knew he was in deep trouble when he began contemplating ways to make it happen. If they were quiet... *No*, he could not have sex in his office. At least not during the workday.

He finally replied: *A tempting offer, but one that could get us both in trouble. However, tonight...I'm all yours. And we can go all. night. long.*

Asia: *I'm leaving work a little early. A quickie before dinner?*

Jamal: *I'm there. Be ready and be naked.*

He powered through the rest of his day. They were meeting Eric and Kathi at the restaurant at seven-thirty and Jamal had locked up and was striding out the door at five on the dot.

Asia's car was in the garage when Jamal arrived home and he started stripping the moment he entered the house. By the time he made it up to the bedroom, he was as naked as his wife, who was lying on the bed with her arms open. He entered her with one deep thrust and set an intense rhythm that shook the bed. She clamped down on him with her inner muscles and he cursed. Electricity shot through his body and he pounded into her harder and faster and she clenched him again and again, demanding that he give her everything. He demanded the same from her and she gave it to him.

"*Jamal!*" Asia screamed out his name as she climaxed all around him.

Jamal threw back his head and exploded in a rush of pleasure that snatched his breath. "I love you."

"I love you, too. I hope we're not going to be late," she said with a tired laugh.

He seriously debated on whether to cancel dinner. In the end, they showered, dressed, and met Eric and Kathi at the restaurant as planned.

Asia and Kathi hugged each other as if they hadn't seen one another in years. Kathi said, "I'm so glad we're finally getting this dinner in."

"Me, too." Asia smiled up at Eric. "Hey, Eric."

After the round of greetings, the two couples conversed until being led to their table. The discussion continued once the drink and food orders had been placed.

"Asia, how was the Afro-Caribbean festival?" Eric asked.

"It was great. The food, the music, the dancing... I've never seen anything like it. I want to go back again to experience the vibe without working, so I can really enjoy it."

Kathi smiled. "We may need to check it out. Speaking of working, how did the article turn out? If it's anything like the one you did on housing discrimination, I know it'll be brilliant."

Asia's eyes lit up. "Thanks. The festival piece will be in the September issue."

The talk paused when the server returned with drinks. They had all ordered wine, except Kathi, who chose lemonade.

Jamal lifted his glass. "I know I'm a little late, but congratulations on the new addition to your family. We wish you many blessings." They all touched glasses. "And to the newest senior writer at *Divine Living & Travel* magazine, my baby."

The table erupted in well wishes and cheers.

"Oh, hell," Eric muttered.

Jamal frowned. "What?" He followed Eric's gaze and cursed under his breath. Of all the restaurants in Los Angeles, why did Stephanie have to choose this one, and tonight?

He hoped she would just go to her table, but he knew it wouldn't be that easy. The woman glared and came straight to their table. He shot a glance at Asia to gauge her response.

"I hope she's not coming over here to start any trouble," Asia said.

Kathi nodded. "Not if she knows what's good for her."

Jamal and Eric shared a glance. Both of their wives had no problems speaking their minds.

"Because of you, I lost my job!" Stephanie yelled as she approached the table, pointing at Jamal. By now, every person in the room had turned their way.

He sighed. "Look, Stephanie—"

Asia hopped up. "*No*. It's because of *you* that you lost your job! Now take your trifling ass away from this table. Don't you ever send me an email or look at my husband again. If you do, I'll make losing your job look like the *best* thing that ever happened to you."

Jamal was on his feet in an instant, his arms wrapped around his wife. Eric had a firm hold on Kathi, who had stood, as well. "It's okay, baby. She's leaving."

The restaurant manager came over. "Is there a problem?"

"Yes," Kathi said. "This woman is harassing my friend."

The man turned toward Stephanie. "Miss, I'm going to have to ask you to leave."

Stephanie looked like she wanted to say something else, but apparently thought better of it and stormed off.

"My apologies for the disturbance," he said.

Jamal nodded. "It's no problem." They all resumed their seats. "Are you okay?" He leaned over and kissed Asia's temple.

"Fine. I'd be better if I could've punched her one good time, though."

"I know that's right." Kathi rolled her eyes. "She must be out of her mind, coming over here like that."

Eric chuckled and rubbed his wife's back. "Relax, Kathi. I don't want you getting upset. Remember the baby."

Asia picked up her wine glass. "I guess I need to be thinking about the same thing, then."

Jamal froze. "What did you just say?"

She slapped a hand over her mouth.

His heart started pounding. "Are you telling me...? Are we...?"

Asia nodded and grinned sheepishly. "Sorry. I was going to tell you tonight after we got home."

It took him a moment to find his voice. "We're having a baby," he whispered, emotion clogging his throat.

"Yep." Smiling, she tilted the glass to her lips.

Jamal reached over and snatched the wine. "What do you think you're doing?"

She giggled. "Oops, my bad."

He shook his head. "Yeah, *yo'* bad."

They all laughed and Eric said, "Well, we're really celebrating tonight. Congratulations. Asia, you have now been relegated to lemonade island with Kathi."

Asia grasped Kathi's hand. "I couldn't be in better company."

Lively chatter ensued, but Jamal was still trying to wrap his mind around the fact that he was going to be a father.

By the time he got home, he was so excited he could hardly contain it. Before he and Asia made in the door good, he had her in his arms. "Do you know how much I love you?"

Asia laid her head on his chest. "I hope it's as much as I love you. Sorry, I sort of ruined the baby surprise."

He chuckled. "Surprise is a good word." He sobered and eased back. "We talked about having children at the beginning, but after things got messed up, I didn't know if you still wanted them. Are you okay with—"

She placed a finger on his lips. "Jamal, I am more than

okay. I am happy, excited, ecstatic...pick one. What about you?"

"I am all of those things and more." Jamal tried to figure out when it could have happened and came to the conclusion that it had been the night she'd left the bed right after. The night that had left him wondering whether his marriage could be salvaged. But he didn't have to wonder any more. He placed a gentle hand on her belly. "Our baby."

Asia covered his hand with hers. *"Ours."*

The kiss that followed was one of affirmation and love. Life was good. And he was never letting her go.

ABOUT THE AUTHOR

Sheryl Lister is a multi-award-winning author and has enjoyed reading and writing for as long as she can remember. She is a former pediatric occupational therapist with over twenty years of experience, and resides in California. Sheryl is a wife, mother of three daughters and a son-in-love, and grandmother to two special little boys. When she's not writing, Sheryl can be found on a date with her husband or in the kitchen creating appetizers. For more information, visit her website at www.sheryllister.com.

instagram.com/sheryllister

ALSO BY SHERYL LISTER

HARLEQUIN KIMANI

Just To Be With You

All Of Me

It's Only You

Be Mine For Christmas (Unwrapping The Holidays Anthology)

Tender Kisses (The Grays of Los Angeles #1)

Places In My Heart (The Grays of Los Angeles #2)

Giving My All To You (The Grays of Los Angeles #3)

A Touch Of Love (The Grays of Los Angeles #4)

Still Loving You (The Grays of Los Angeles #5)

His Los Angeles Surprise

A Love Of My Own (The Hunters Of Sacramento #1)

Sweet Love (The Hunters Of Sacramento #2)

Spark Of Desire (The Hunters Of Sacramento #3)

Designed By Love (The Hunters Of Sacramento #4)

OTHER TITLES

Made To Love You

It's You That I Need

Perfect Chemistry

Embracing Forever (Once Upon A Bridesmaid #3)

Love's Serenade (Decades: A Journey Of African American
Romance #3)

Sweet Summer Days

The Reluctant Bid

Closer To You

Made in the USA
Las Vegas, NV
25 August 2021